THE WEATHERING

THE WEATHERING

ARTEM CHAPEYE

TRANSLATED BY DAISY GIBBONS

SEVEN STORIES PRESS
New York • Oakland

Originally published in Ukrainian as Вивітрювання by "21-Publishers" (Видавництво 21) in 2021.

Seven Stories Press
140 Watts Street
New York, NY 10013
www.sevenstories.com

LIBRARY OF CONGRESS CATALOGING-IN-PUBLICATION DATA

Names: Chapaĭ, Artem author | Gibbons, Daisy translator
Title: The weathering : a novel / Artem Chapeye translated by Daisy Gibbons.
Other titles: Vyvitriuvannia. English
Description: New York : Seven Stories Press, 2026.
Identifiers: LCCN 2025051254 (print) | LCCN 2025051255 (ebook) | ISBN 9781644215463 trade paperback | ISBN 9781644215470 ebook
Subjects: LCGFT: Apocalyptic fiction | Novels | Fiction
Classification: LCC PG3950.13.H37 V9813 2026 (print) | LCC PG3950.13.H37 (ebook)
LC record available at https://lccn.loc.gov/2025051254
LC ebook record available at https://lccn.loc.gov/2025051255

College professors and high school and middle school teachers may order free examination copies of Seven Stories Press titles. Visit https://www.sevenstories.com/pg/resources-academics or email academic@sevenstories.com.

Printed in the United States of America

9 8 7 6 5 4 3 2 1

Contents

Author's Note on the English Translation

I maintain the belief that an author should not offer interpretations of their own text. Nonetheless, it became clear during the editing of the English translation of this book that it might be helpful for the reader to have additional information.

The Ukrainian edition of *The Weathering* was released in mid-2021, half a year before Russia's full-scale invasion of Ukraine. Therefore, references to the war in this novel and its effect on the fate of certain characters have little to do with my gift of prophecy and rather much to do with the armed aggression that Russia launched against Ukraine in 2014. But that's not all.

The observant editor of this book and my earlier works in English translation, *The Ukraine* and *Ordinary People Don't Carry Machine Guns,* noticed that certain themes, characters, and places appear and reappear in the texts. I hope that similarly observant readers will also notice recurring details in future translations of my books. When I was an adolescent, I was blown away by literature with imagined, populated multiverses, such as those by Jules Verne, William Faulker, or Gabriel García Márquez—to name the first few authors that come to mind. Indeed, the location in the early chapters of *The Weathering* is the same as in a story in *The*

Ukraine, which I wrote when my wife was pregnant in 2012. Nevertheless, what is more important than time and place is theme.

The same observant reader will notice how events reverberate through the book, events that happened not only in Ukraine but—this point I must emphasize—the whole world; like the pandemic, for instance, which, as its Greek prefix *pan-* meaning "all" indicates, really was worldwide. As such, places all over the globe—from Libya to Syria, Tasmania, Madagascar, Ireland, and the place that "even after the end of the world . . . must remain the center of the end of the world"—are mentioned, explicitly or implicitly, in the novel.

Why do I stress the theme of universality? In Orhan Pamuk's novel *Snow,* a Kurdish poet remarks that when a German poet writes poetry, he supposedly speaks on behalf of all humanity, but "when we write something, it is just 'ethnic poetry.'" No—it is finally time to acknowledge that any literature, not only literature written in the several major world languages, speaks universally about the human condition. The Ukrainian author writes not only about Ukraine but about *all* humanity, just as the Congolese, Bangladeshi, or Palestinian writer does.

While I am here, I will use the opportunity to express deep gratitude to my agent, Emma Shercliff, who did more than anyone to promote the translation of my Ukrainian books into English. Likewise, I express thanks to the editorial staff at *The New Yorker* for publishing my story in 2022 in solidarity with all of Ukraine, and who gave us support at a crucial moment in those first weeks of the Russian invasion, when I joined the army and my wife and children became refugees, and I had no idea how they would survive. I also have been very fortunate with Seven Stories Press, and I would like to express my special gratitude to Ruth Weiner for her thoroughness: We edited and proofread this translation more times, it seems, than I did the original; although there was more to it than editing, of course. The English-language text that you are about to read has a coauthor, translator Daisy Gibbons, someone whom I have known for I cannot remember how long, and who, unexpectedly to her it seems, is becoming a star of Ukrainian-to-English literary translation. (Daisy, thank you also for the flowers for my wife.) I consider it a correct practice to put a translator's name directly onto a book cover. After all, there are many literatures in many languages in the world, and it is the translator who turns each from "ethnic" to "world" literature.

KYIV CITY CENTER
Ukraine

1 • **RUSANIVKA ISLAND**
2 • **HYDROPARK** (on the Truhaniv archipelago)
3 • **KYIV-PECHERSK LAVRA** (visible from Rusanivka)
4 • **ROADS TO MOUNTAINS** (West)
5 • **DNIPRO RIVER FLOW** (North to South)

2
1
5
1 mile/1.6 kilometers
0
.5
1
N

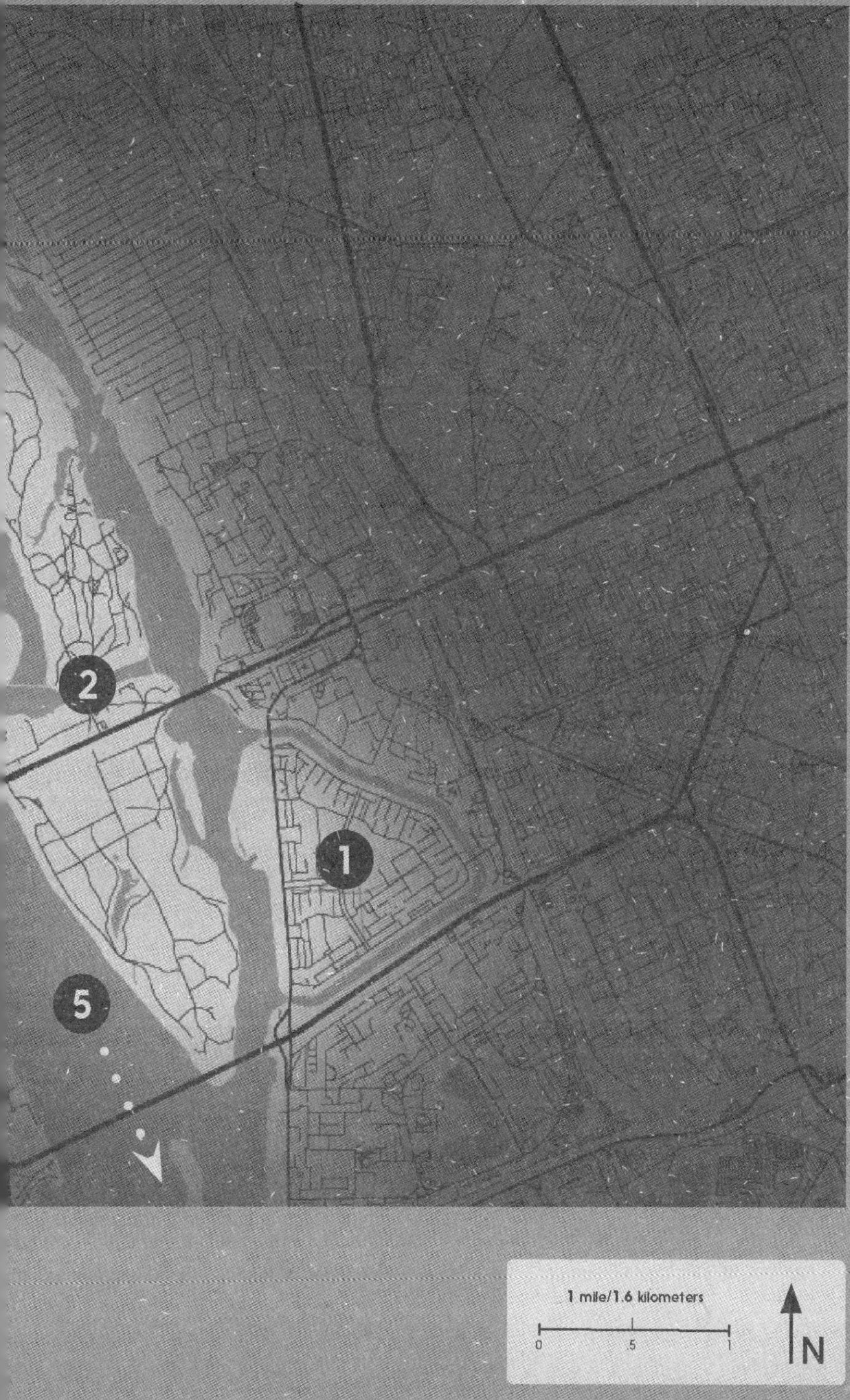

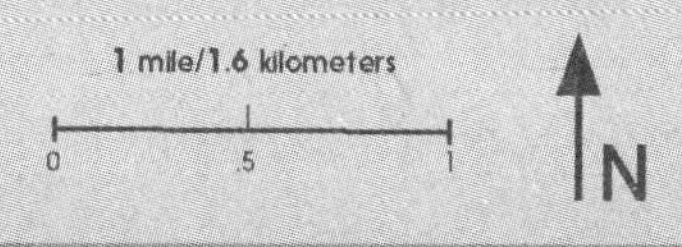

MOUNTAIN

1

The two of us, Zoïa and I, were dog tired.

For the past few years, we had been working two-and-a-half jobs each. An office job, a work-from-home job, and another side gig. All of our temporary and unstable work we referred to as freelance. Because, you know, we practically do it for free.

"Almost sounds dignified, the word 'freelance,' even if we are really scrabbling for scraps," Zoïa said.

We had both left our humble beginnings in the Ukrainian countryside to make new humble beginnings in the capital, Kyiv, where we entered university. We started working alongside our studies to save for our own flat. Rent ate up most of what we'd set aside. We comforted ourselves with rumors off the internet that, in some cities, people live their whole lives this way.

"What did you expect? Kyiv's the new Berlin," said Zoïa, then snorted into her coffee.

One day, we decided to count how much we had saved up since we were teenagers. Our sanity perished with the realization.

Zoïa perched on the balcony, rocking and making an 'O' with her fingers.

"One does not simply get a flat in Kyiv. Not through honest work. You need someone else's money, an inheritance or help. And associating with Ukrainian banks is practically taboo. We're not in Europe, *tsenk you very mach*, even if we are the new Berlin. You know, when one of my friends from university hit thirty and we asked him what his greatest achievement was, he just said, 'I'm not in debt.' We're still young but we've lived through crisis after crisis—national and international. One just rolls into the next in those terrains."

What would happen next? The two of us, Zoïa and I, were unprepared for that. We had to take a break.

We had to recalibrate, as Zoïa put it.

In the beginning of June, we both took unpaid leave (as dictated by the chivalric code of the realm of the freelancer), went to our landlords in their nice downtown neighborhood and paid for two months' rent up front, turned off our gas and water, and before dawn one day we got in our car, the trusty Raquel—a second-hand gray Daewoo Lanos that ran on the cheapest gas—and set off towards the Carpathian Mountains.

Raquel, the old mare, got into her stride after we passed Zhytomyr. But then the acceleration cut out. A dull thud and we lost power. No matter how hard I pressed my foot on the gas, the revs kept falling, and Raquel died.

"What, again?" said Zoïa, apathetically.

"Christ's sake. We haven't even done a thousand k yet."

"Ah yes! Didn't you say last week, 'Funny, the car hasn't broken down in a while'?"

I laughed, nervous.

I climbed out and lifted the bonnet. Ah. As expected: The O-ring had come off. Piece of shit. It's this little rubber ring that covers the mixer system connecting the engine to the fuel tank. I think. It had been less than a month since it was last changed. Maybe there really was something wrong with my driving. The ring had pinged off so many times that even I knew what to do: seal the joint up with a bandage from the first aid kit, then drive to the nearest garage.

"Is that safe?"

"Devil knows."

Nowhere was open yet. Only the birds in the forest lining the road were awake with a busy twittering.

We stopped for repairs in Radyvyliv nearly 300 km later. A young lad in oil-stained coveralls silently installed a new rubber ring. A routine procedure.

"What you doin' that it keeps comin' off then?" he looked at me with pity, as practical guys look at helpless intellectuals.

Then, when we passed Stryi another 180 km later, the damn drive shaft came loose. This is the part that connects the gearbox to the wheels. I think. This time, I was most certainly to blame for maiming our dear Raquel. I had been stuck behind three trucks on a winding road and there was no way in hell I could get past; I trailed them for half an hour until I finally lost my temper and, while conducting a flash overtake, I must have shifted into a lower gear too abruptly without pressing on the clutch or taking my foot off the gas. I might even have switched the gearstick into reverse while moving. I've done that before: muscle memory kicks in and I act without thinking. The old mare's ball joints started to grind and come loose; then, her bones started rattling terribly, poor old Raquel shuddered with pain and limped onto the hard shoulder—and that was the end. She lay there, not breathing.

Thank God we did not cause an accident.

Zoïa said nothing. I knew this state of hers, what she called her ice-cold fury. I just sniffed and kept silent, to avoid an argument.

We waited on the roadside and we watched the trucks. Every time I bypass Stryi on the motorway, I am always struck by the reams of dust thrown up by caravans of heavy vehicles. The trucks seem to congregate here, gaggling into herds that stretch on and on like the great migration on the African savanna I saw on National Geographic. Only these cows never stop flowing past, on and on and on.

A nice man in an old-school, cherry-red Lada towed Raquel to a garage, then refused to accept any money. By then it was lunchtime, and the repairs took the remains of the day. The kind old uncle at the garage phoned around for new ball joints, drove to Stryi, bought them, and then kept working until the car was fixed, which was after dark. We gratefully slipped him a few extra notes when he gave us the bill.

"Enough. We should relax now and spend the night here," Zoïa sighed, then stroked my neck. I flinched from the unexpected contact to my clammy skin, but I was grateful to Zoïa for this deliberate, even forced, sign of tenderness.

"Sure," I replied.

The word "relax" was said with tension. We needed to recalibrate—again. We were suffering from chronic fatigue. The kind of fatigue you can't overcome with a good night's sleep. You can't recover from it over a weekend, or even a week of rest.

Tomorrow, though. Tomorrow we would travel slow and steady, just like that: slo-o-ow and steady. Meditatively. Just breathing deeply if something goes awry.

Besides, tomorrow we'd no longer be driving on paved road, and it's best to avoid the dirt roads after dark, which is why we made a healthy detour around Stryi to stay on the tarmac for as long as we could. A while back, I attempted to turn off at Dubno for Kolomyia, going via Ternopil and Horodenka out in the sticks of western Ukraine, my home. A risky business. As one of my old schoolfriends put it, "Just picturing the roads there is enough to send me in the other direction." That one time, caught on a dirt track in a deep, thick fog, I encountered a magnificent mechanical farm beast that looked like a diplodocus, melancholically chewing plant stems and lumbering across the beat-up track from one edge to the other. I was extremely lucky to push through at 20 km after that, meandering around the potholes in the fog. No, not again. Better the dusty detour. Even if the detour means being lost among the herds of trucks around Stryi.

We spent the night in a tacky "pay-by-the-hour-chic" motel, as Zoïa put it. The room had a mirror covering the whole wall, sequined wallpaper, and three condoms in pink wrappers on the bedside table.

"Ooooh!" cooed Zoïa, reaching after them in pure jest: we were already fucked without the sex.

The trucks rumbled, honked, and hissed outside the window. Its exterior glass pane was coated in a thick layer of dust.

We left at four thirty in the morning. We could hear the scream of lung-bursting birdsong in the lulls between trucks. We drove on in a melancholy mood, taking our time, listening to Tom Waits, and did not hit a single pothole. Raquel didn't start sneezing or limping or sagging, and so Zoïa and I could turn our attention to the beauty of the misty blue mountains on our approach. They parted before us and closed behind us, and by noon we arrived without incident.

"Praise Jesus! I was expectin' yous yesterday."

The gruff voice with its highlander accent belonged to Uncle Vasyl. He greeted us as he came out the gate.

"The car broke down."

"Agh no, let the devil eat 'em both," Vasyl sympathized abstractly, not putting much feeling into the esoteric expression. "But still. Yer made it."

"Yep, wer made it," I replied.

Vasyl opened the gate of the fence made from long, narrow, smooth planks of pine stacked horizontally. Or were they spruce? A shaggy, dirty-white dog that looked like a polar bear from a video about climate change jumped out to greet us, but was restrained by the thick chain around its neck. Vasyl shooed him away.

"Oi, Overko, back in the doghouse wit yer!"

Around the hut, in a radius the same length of the chain, the grass was trampled "to nowt," as they say in these parts. Well-trodden paths led from the house to the barn, and to the road.

The rest of the grass in the large yard was a juicy green, neatly mowed. The horse and livestock grazed further up the mountain.

"Wer made it," Zoïa said. Stepping on the soft grass, she inhaled deeply and held her breath. A pause. "And . . . exhale."

2

I stood in the yard breathing deeply and silently. Zoïa came up to me and took my hand without a word. I lifted my head to the sky and closed my eyes to cast out thoughts of the city, politics, the thousand-and-one things on my to-do list, to forget the journey, the noise of the trucks, the dusty potholes.

Further up the mountain, copper bells were clanging. A sheep bleated. The smell of cattle, moist hay, dew, and pine needles.

"We going up that mountain there now? Or we stayin' the night in the village?"

Zoïa and I looked at each other. We had to get back into the car—if only for the last stretch. Ugh.

"Is the place ready for us?"

"Aye so it is. I were expectin' yous yesterday."

"Let's go today," Zoïa decided. "But let's swing by the shop first."

"Ah, hang on, my ol' lady will feed yous first. We're not settin' off right now."

"Vasyl . . . I'm sorry to ask, but you don't happen to have any of that delicious sheep's cheese, what's it called?

He chuckled.

"Oh, the *budz*? Aye, so we do. Like I said, we were expectin' yous."

His wife, Maria, a short, squat woman with shorter gray hair, silently fed us heavenly fried potatoes with creamy, salty *budz*. She then went out to silently feed the pigs. Zoïa, wry as ever, couldn't help but note the parallel between us and the pigs. Just to me, of course.

Meanwhile Uncle Vasyl packed up. We went to the sty to thank Maria and say goodbye. She waved and said the first words we'd heard her say: "God be with you." We saddled Raquel again. I was still licking my lips, but I didn't have the nerve to ask Vasyl whether they always eat so well or if this was only for us tourists.

We drove up through the village at a glacial pace, so that the great boulders sticking out of the road would not scrape the undercarriage. The boulders had emerged because the rainwater was constantly washing away the tracks. Thankfully, the soil was rocky, which slows erosion. "Erosion" is Latin. *What would be the native Ukrainian word?* I wondered as I sought a level path over the road. Would it be *vyvitriuvannia*, like the Anglo-Saxon "weathering"? *But the meaning is slightly different*, thought one side of my brain to the other as the rest of me drove one of the car tires over a small boulder slowly, very slowly, so as to not beach the car. We gently see-sawed over the lump of rock like a ship cresting and falling over an ocean wave. *Where erosion moves rocks and dirt from one place to another, weathering is a more invisible, gradual vanishing.* Which Ukrainian roads are a good example of . . . Dammit! I cursed under my breath as a boulder hit the undercarriage of the car. Inevitable!

Vasyl's brother-in-law ran the village shop next to the brook. The shop was a dark room in a rain-blackened wooden house. Sacks of grain, boxes of winter onions, Ukrainian sodas, and six-packs of two-liter bottles of Coke in plastic cases stood on the floor. Zoïa and I bought one bottle of vodka and a lot of little chocolates. Painkillers are necessary in the mountains sometimes. Well. Not just in the mountains.

Vasyl was waiting by Raquel.

"Yous ready? Hang on, jus' let me smoke up. Don' want to stop later."

I suddenly had a desperate urge for a cigarette. The two of us, Zoïa and I, had quit when we decided to try for a baby. True, we were still baby-less, but we weren't going to resume the habit. If I did, Zoïa would too. Fortunately, Vasyl only had one cigarette left, so the sudden urge passed just as suddenly. Vasyl crumpled the cigarette packet and carelessly tossed it into the brook.

"*Dyadko* Vasyl!" Zoïa gasped. She never had learnt how to say *vuiko*, which is what people in western Ukraine call their uncles and other older males of uncertain relation. She always used the eastern *dyadko*. She grew up on the "Left Bank," east of the river Dnipro. "But this is where you live!"

It took Vasyl a moment to understand what she meant.

"The water washes it all away."

"No, it doesn't! Look at the riverbank!"

The banks of the brook were littered with pink and light green plastic bags, tarnished tin cans, and fluorescent blue biscuit wrappers. Hm. Maybe people here hadn't realized that waste is different nowadays, compared to when the water used to "wash it all away." Seven or eight years ago, Zoïa and I went to Svaneti, in Georgia. The steep ravine down to the river in the mountain town of Mestia was strewn with litter. There we saw an old lady, wrapped in a headscarf, bent double with a walking stick, throw a whole sack of refuse off the ravine edge and walk off without stopping.

That's what I remembered. Zoïa had quite a different story for Vasyl: "*Dyadko* Vasyl, we stayed in a mountain resort recently. Dzembronya, you know it, it's not far from here. But the people there sort their trash! They collect the plastic and take it all the way to the district town whenever someone has to go down to the valley."

"Oh aye, good for them. I keep my own backyard clean," he replied. "Cause it's mine, see. C'mon . . . you tree-hugging Greta."

"Please don't be offended."

"Weren't planning on it," he laughed.

But he didn't speak the whole way to the mountain hut. I didn't see where he put the cigarette butt.

The road out of the village grew steeper and steeper. Raquel, the old mare, could barely make the last ten meters; she's not a Jeep, after all. The road became much smoother immediately after we left the village, and the ruts were not as deep. We drove through tall grass along the mountain ridge, where the tops of pine trees on the slopes on either side barely reached us. Gradually, the blue mountains opened ahead. They really are blue here. It's not just a name.

We slowly climbed higher and higher. You don't see many cars this high up: there's nowhere for them to go. Just horse-drawn carts from here on. That's why there is no evidence of erosion here, merely trampled grass. We pushed through the tops of the pines first, then rose above them. The horizon revealed itself, and at the next turn we could see the village far below. We had been suddenly propelled up, lifted up on high by the wind's currents: there we were, flying in our airship, *La Raquelle,* over a painted map, leaping over the patches of light and the shadows thrown by the hills below, and all around us were mountain peaks covered in navy forests or otherwise faded yellow and bare. There were no precipices, no rock faces; everything was smooth and rounded, every hill marked by a footpath leading to their apogee. Here the Carpathians are rolling, peaceful, intimate.

There was no more wind after we climbed higher. The road—essentially two soft parallel paths in the grass—bisected two mountains along a saddle ridge. We opened the windows as we sailed along at walking pace. On both sides the grass was so green and fresh that it shone. A grasshopper was perched on every blade. There were two hundred different shades of these insects, from a light lettuce-green to a dark chestnut. Startled by Raquel, the grasshoppers fled, drawing wide arcs in the air. One landed on Zoïa's shoulder.

"It's rare you enter a dreamscape like this in a Daewoo Lanos," I said.

"Which is good," replied Zoïa.

The place was removed from the famous tourist trails. None of the highest peaks for anyone to "conquer" were nearby, only ones of middling height. Far to our left, Petros peak protruded. That's where the hikers go. The rounded dome of Sheshul was closer. People go there less often. Our location was a few hundred meters lower in altitude, so not as interesting. And the road leads nowhere, a natural dead end of steep slopes densely forested with spruce, firs, and pine. The old names for the peaks around here didn't even show up on maps until smartphones came about. Web maps still show different names for some of them. Some time ago, I personally named one of the smaller mountains on a hiking app. I checked the route with Vasyl, climbed to the top, marked the place on the app, and gave it a name.

True, when I asked our inside man for the local name, Vasyl answered with uncertainty, jokingly invented a name on the spot, and then added, "Why do we need to name every hilltop anyhow?"

So, I'm still unsure whether I climbed and named the right hill.

The highest peak in this area—the round-topped mountain we were traversing up in our Daewoo—has several names, just like Sagarmatha-Everest-Chomolungma, but an unknown, miniature version. To my and Zoïa's delight, we noted the local curiousity of place names ending in *-os* or *-ul.* I made a mental note to ask or read up on why that is.

I will probably never find out now.

3

We curved up and around the mountain. We reached a hollow tucked above a stream, where the little hut that we were renting now for the third time stood. Vasyl seemed delighted that we were spending the whole summer here on this occasion. More convenient for him: fewer people wandering through the village who might attract attention. The wooden hut was actually a high-altitude research station belonging to the state, but it hadn't been used for several years. Funding for expeditions had disappeared after yet another economic crisis. Vasyl stopped getting paid to be its caretaker, so he quietly started renting the place out to "trusted people."

We parked Raquel in the recess between the house and the dugout and a fortified slope beside it. That way the car wasn't visible from the outside.

"You remember where the commode is," Vasyl waved at a wooden outhouse. "Wood's over there, should be enough fer two months. Even if yer wanted to light a fire erryday," he explained. "Right, in here next."

He unlocked the padlock hanging from the cellar hatch. The door was overgrown with emerald moss. The cellar was dank and sodden. Water oozed out of the clay-daubed walls, probably the same water that runs into the mountain stream below. We climbed down. Each of the concrete steps was steep, knee-height.

"Yer got beetroot, carrots, should be enough to last . . . Some pig fat in this jar here, look. And this," said Vasyl, pointing at the stacks of cans wrapped in plastic wrap on a rough shelf, "is some canned meat. Yer 'strategic reserve.'"

"No way! Is this taken from a Soviet nuclear bunker?"

"Ha-ha. No, they're Polish."

"What? You mean the cans are pre-World War II?"

For a second, Vasyl gaped at me in astonishment.

"It's fresh—I jus' brought it over the border! Who do you take me fer?"

"Oh. Sorry. Just the way you said 'strategic reserve' . . ."

Vasyl shook his head, laughing. He showed us what was where in the pantry and in the house. Tea, coffee, sugar, salt, pepper, matches. Even a pack of Prima cigarettes, Ukraine's cheapest—although the "De Luxe" sort. If the craving hit.

We agreed with Vasyl that he would swing by every two weeks to check on us and to bring fresh herbs and vegetables, or anything else that wouldn't keep for months. I didn't want to trouble him, but it was not like we were asking for fresh olives and mozzarella, as Zoïa put it. It's just so we weren't surviving on salo and buckwheat.

Ice-cold water came from the stream. If we wanted to bathe, we had to fill up a black metal tub the night before and hope the sun would warm it up. Then again, we were used to surviving half the summer without hot water in Kyiv due to the gas shortages (and the flat isn't ours, so all the Boiler Evangelists out there can save their speeches on us, because we can't install one). So, an evening tub of lukewarm water in the mountains was not too bad. If it happened to be cold and rainy, we could always fire up the trusty old kettle. Just like we do in our modern, European capital city.

There was no electricity at the old high-altitude research station, obviously. Nor was there mobile internet coverage. If we needed to call someone, we would have to traverse around and up the mountain to get reception. In other words, all was exactly how we wanted it. Back home, Zoïa was always calling people and solving problems for her work. I had to monitor the news and be contactable 24/7. And, of course, the doom scrolling. Here, amid the mountains, we could turn everything off. We could build up our energy. We had fully charged our phones back in the tacky, pay-by-the-hour-chic motel and, in case of emergencies, we had a few external batteries. We'd filled Raquel up to the brim with gas at the last station before the climb up to Vasyl's village.

I had brought a book collection of everything I could read again for the thousandth time: all of Kawabata in translation, Orhan Pamuk's *Snow*, Conrad's *Heart of Darkness*, and Chekhov's later prose, written after he had come to know all the vagaries of existence in researching the Sakhalin Katorga. Zoïa's gold standard was Jane Austen and the Strugatsky brothers' sci-fi novels. I could borrow her copy of *The Doomed City.* Who knows how much we would actually read. But the presence of the books was warming. Like carrying a thick sweater on an autumn hike, even if it stays in your rucksack.

We did not know what we were going to do. Let summer run its course. The slower, the better. As companions who realized in adulthood that we were both introverts, we would not get bored. "Only let's not delve into our problems," Zoïa had said. "Our minds can rest, and solutions will emerge."

Or not.

"Jus' look after the place, so I don't get no problems," Uncle Vasyl said as he left.

"We won't burn it down," Zoïa replied sunnily.

"Jest don' go and do anythin' daft. An ambulance will take a long time gettin' up here, you know."

"Yes, of course! I remember your bear stories," I said, trying to take the sting out of Zoïa's sarcasm.

"That's the badger. Behave yerselves, you two."

"We'll behave," Zoïa affirmed.

Vasyl gave me a firm handshake. His palm could have been made of wood it was so much harder than mine. Uncle Vasyl merely nodded at Zoïa. Kindly, to be fair to him. He turned around, walked down into the valley, and we never saw him again.

We were left alone together.

I felt the need to breathe slowly and deeply.

I closed my eyes.

The stream trickled below and the pines creaked above us. Sunspots flickered across my eyelids. The breeze skimmed over my face. I could make out the distinct fragrances of moist moss and warm, dry pine needles.

Zoïa ran her fingertips with a soft rustle over the short hair on the back of my head.

"Let's go. Time to misbehave."

4

Three weeks passed. In the mornings we heated the water up in the iron tub on the stove. We washed together, standing barefoot between Raquel and the forest. The dark forest wall loomed nearby, just a few meters from the house.

The rough-barked trunks of the conifers stood high, and the edges of the forest canopy floated above. The fallen needles pricked our bare feet. Over the past few weeks, the gray roof and bonnet of the car had gradually acquired a fine blanket of spruce needles.

Without getting dressed, Zoïa and I would go into the house and for hours, prolonging every caress, we made love. As we lay afterwards, embracing, she and I watched specks of dust playing in the light, our skin warmed by the slanting rays of the sun as it shone on the iron bed, so like the one I slept in during summer holidays in my grandfather's village. Across a small window there, Grandpa had stretched a fishing wire between two nails hammered into the wooden window frame, where a net curtain hung, embroidered, white on white, with deer and fawns flitting between fir trees. The fishing wire passed through little holes embroidered in the shape of birds. A small wooden bookstand stood by the wall in front of the bed. There was only a handful of books on the shelf. They included the Bible that my grandfather would reread constantly, despite not attending church on principle because, he said, he didn't trust the clergy. Next to it, in the same faux-leather binding and same shade of black was the Soviet *Refuting the Bible*, Politpress, 1965 edition. There was *Edible and Poisonous Mushrooms of Ukraine* from 1970, with faded color illustrations. Then, out of character, Clifford D. Simak's sci-fi novel *City*, a relatively recent publication, post-perestroika. My father probably left it the last time he went there.

Newspapers, new and old, also lay on every shelf of the bookcase. They were like the editions I would read and reread over the blissful, endless vacation weeks of my childhood. These were from the winter of '92 to '93. The year my mother and I stood for milk and bread in seemingly endless lines. I hadn't realized so many people lived in our neighborhood. So many that a crowd gathered even beyond the threshold of the shop's glass doors. I hadn't yet felt the severe cold, but my legs were frozen to the bone. But when we got to the front of the line, my mother wasted our treasured coupon stamps that she would cut off with little scissors she carried for that function. Wasted them on me. We had noticed a plastic figurine of Donald Duck on the counter. It was unclear from where it had appeared in this grocery shop on the outskirts of a just-post-Soviet country town, and my mom bought it for me. I clutched the Donald toy tight in my fist and I was happy. When my mother and I came back from the shop and my chilblained legs thawed out, I whimpered from the pain, squeezing the little Donald Duck toy in my hand. Yet this newspaper from the same period of deprivation lying on my grandfather's shelf had a full page devoted, incredibly, to an advertisement for an Alfa Romeo automobile for anyone and everyone who wanted to—I quote—"excite their sensuality and satisfy any whim." It also invited any passing reader to work as a car dealer.

Probably it was the same winter when my granny made us tea from cherry twigs in her snow-covered garden. Granny went outside into the cherry orchard blanketed in fluffy snow, and I looked out the window, my back against the ancient, ceramic-tiled peasant stove, and watched her walk through the depths, getting smaller and smaller as she hopped away from us through the snow like an old-timey schoolgirl. Everything from before I was born was old-timey to me then. Then the tiny schoolgirl returned, getting bigger and turning back into my granny, lifting her knees up high under her stiff skirt, galoshes over her felt winter boots, holding a bundle in her fist. My granny entered the hut, stamping snow everywhere and emitting the smell of cold, and took off her galoshes. A dozen fine cherry twigs were in her hand. I don't know exactly how she steamed the twigs, but I can still remember the viscous smell to this day. My madeleines.

"What are you thinking about?"

Zoïa brought me back to myself.

"Nothing really . . . Everything."

Zoïa lay her head on my shoulder. I stroked her belly with my free hand and had a sudden desperate urge to inspect it, inspect the soft, golden down in the slanting rays of sunlight, the sun-touched, tan skin that shone brown. I brushed my hand over it. I thought how smooth her belly looked, how beautifully it curved when Zoïa arched her back to cuddle in closer to me. And how hot it was, too.

By the time we made it outside, it was already the next day.

From the hut you have to scramble up a steep path for twenty meters or so before reaching the smooth upward path that spirals around our round-topped mountain. After so much love, a cloud floated in my stomach and my feet felt like they were made of rubber. Walking did not feel like walking but hovering. We moved slowly so as not to dilute our enjoyment.

"It seems like Vasyl hasn't been round in a while," Zoïa finally said.

"We can phone him from the high moor," I answered lazily. "Phone reception's better somewhere up there."

"Eh, we don't have to. I just suddenly had a craving for cucumbers. I'll get over it."

"We'll just drop a hint, like, 'How's the wife, how're the animals and the farm?' The usual opening lines. Then ask, 'By the way, how are the cucumbers coming up?'"

Zoïa giggled.

"He's going to know the moment he picks up the phone why us hungry tourists are calling him."

"Anyway, we didn't bring our phones today."

"Well, this too."

We moved uphill without speaking. I also suddenly wanted something juicy to crunch on. But not enough to phone Vasyl and burst our bubble of isolation. I had known Uncle Vasyl for about seven years before Zoïa and I first started coming here, and he always maintained the impression of a responsible person. He would not forget us.

The two of us, Zoïa and I, phoned my mother and Zoïa's parents a few times at the beginning, but then we turned off our phones. Two or three times I thought to call my mother to tell her we were ok, but then I always forgot. My mother, touch wood, is in good health. True, something could always happen. But if it happened suddenly, then we'd never get there in time. And if it wasn't sudden, then we would make it.

Or not.

Zoïa and I circled the hill counterclockwise along a narrow path, in single file. I tried to breathe evenly and slowly, I wanted to preserve the feeling of lightness in my legs and especially the cloud in my stomach, just below my diaphragm. We breathed easily. It was good we had quit smoking. I saw how delicately Zoïa stepped along the path and I found myself wanting her again, though strictly in my mind for now. In the mountains I had become easily excitable, like a teenager. Well. No wonder, without the legions of tasks and legions of restless thoughts. The days were long. When Zoïa didn't want to go on a hike, I would go myself. I didn't even read.

The horizon dipped and spread out convex beneath us like a football turned inside out. From our domed peak, the view opened onto what must have been dozens of kilometers: forests and hoary tufts of clouds beneath our feet. And it felt like, as far as we could see, there was not a single person down there.

Maybe that was so. Even by then.

We returned when the sky started to darken. The two of us, Zoïa and I, agreed that dusk in the mountains is blue. This color deepens into violet then quietly congeals into blackness, after which the galaxy emerges across the sky.

I lit a fire that burned orange in the house. The cold arrives quickly in the mountains, even after warm days. In Kyiv, brisk changes in weather happen only in October and November. Here, we sometimes woke up to light frost. Once or twice even snow. But it was peaceful in the hut. When the wood had burned up, I opened the grate and watched the dark-orange embers wander across the dark canvas, as on the Sun. When I was a kid, I thought this was lava. It fascinated me.

Zoïa and I drank tea from enamel tin mugs. The ones that are white with a black rim and are always chipped for some reason. The edges of these mugs are always hot, but this has its own sort of pleasure. We touched our lips to them carefully, slurping slowly. Pouting our lips together, like children do for a kiss.

And then we would kiss with burning lips. I cannot even remember the last time over the years of the rat race in Kyiv, when we had the time and inclination for a real, long kiss, not during sex.

There was no artificial light. We made a second cup of tea each and sat on the rough wooden threshold—a thick, cracked, rectangular beam. We leaned against one another. Above the spiky pine trees the feathering of the Milky Way hung over half the sky. And when, during those Kyiv rat race years, was the last time I gazed so long, so consciously, at the night sky? I have been fascinated by space since childhood. Zoïa said I was a cosmophile, to use the expression used by her beloved Strugatsky brothers. But so what? As a child, you dream of planting apple orchards on Mars and then you get older and your dream shrinks to buying a studio apartment in Kyiv. To have a slower pace of life, apparently. It disgusts me, feeling like Alice running as fast as she can to stay in the same place, and running twice as fast to get anywhere else. Those are all the apple orchards on Mars you're gonna get, kid.

I thought about saying all this to Zoïa, but then I changed my mind. I didn't want to spoil the moment for her.

"Today's been so long," said Zoïa.

"I know. It's great."

"I couldn't live like this all the time."

"Well, sure . . ."

We didn't need to say anything else. I lowered my hand from her waist to the rough threshold. The wooden beam had dried out. Slowly leading my hand along the fibers, I felt the welts where the wood had weathered away over the years.

"Should we drink up and go to bed?" Zoïa proposed lazily.

I sighed. "How about another cup of tea? I'll make it."

Zoïa laughed, and it was like silver.

"Space-watching?" She nodded towards the metallic dusting of the galaxy above the black matte triangles of the pines. "You have one. I don't want another. I'll just sit with you. Bring the blanket, though."

I brought everything, put the blanket over her shoulders and slurped my black tea. The smell of dry wood and earthen floor. The tip of my nose felt the cold.

In the darkness something groaned. Then whimpered.

Suddenly the pines creaked. A weather front passing through, it seemed like. A bat fluttered gently above. And then it disappeared. A flock of tiny birds flew past with a whistle of their wings. Why at night?

Something was going on.

There was a light throbbing in my chest. It was pleasant enough. I was lightheaded, too. Probably all the lovemaking this morning. I poured out the thick brew of tea leaves left at the bottom of my mug onto the pine needles. The dark forest wall loomed nearby.

5

"Haven't seen any stray tourists lately."

"Good," I laughed.

For the first couple of weeks, someone would walk past us once every two or three days. Some were lost, others had deliberately strayed from known paths. A few times we saw what looked like people dotted in the dips between neighboring peaks.

Then it rained for a long time. Streaks of fog gathered whenever it stopped. Zoïa would not leave the house for three days. Her e-reader's battery nearly went dead. I read less than I expected to.

When the wind died down, I would grab my rubber boots and plastic raincoat and hike. I had to stride slowly to not sweat too much. The rain gently pattered on the hood of my raincoat, creating a meditative ambience. I waded on and on, and the sloping grass quietly rustled against my boots. When the water from the sky stopped or eased off to a drizzle, I could throw back my hood. My wet hair stuck to my forehead. But it was all so peaceful. While the downpour lasted it got tiring, always looking at the ground to stop the rain from getting in my eyes. So, I turned into the forest. The forest was too dense to walk straight through, tangled bushes that you could not clear. But there were tracks. The pine needles underfoot were waterlogged. It was like walking on a sodden rug.

The branches growing crosswise over the path slapped wetly at my raincoat. If I let my guard down, I got a lusty slap on my bare face. Which is why as soon as the wind and the rain subsided, I returned to the high moor. A film of cold and wet covered my face, but inside my raincoat was relatively warm and dry. Knowing I could always return to a warm stove, some hot tea, a quick bath and, without toweling down or getting dressed, get straight into a snug, dry bed next to Zoïa, was especially comforting.

At last, the sun started to peek through. A milky fog floated beneath our feet and flooded the valleys. Only the mountain tops protruded beneath a washed-out sky. A few days later the high moors dried out a little. The two of us, Zoïa and I, started going out again. After the rain, the hikers stopped coming. Maybe there was some crisis down in the valleys. Another Covid lockdown, perhaps, or another transport network collapse. Maybe everyone was scared off by the prolonged rains. Or maybe, was my lazy assumption, in the valley, under the thick fog that people below thought were clouds, they still had rain and thought we did too.

The two of us, Zoïa and I, slowly climbed over the cleft in the mountain ridge, at the bottom of which snow lay when we arrived in June. Now the warm water from the skies had melted and washed it away. While walking along the path running along the forest's upper edge, we disturbed small stones, which tumbled down a steep slope, down between the pines. The landscape on this side looked volcanic. Somehow un-Carpathian. Below, the pines and juniper halted the soil erosion.

The conifers do not grow as densely here as further down, below our hut, where the forest suffocates the smaller vegetation below it. Here, on the slopes, there was enough light between the fir trees for thick, lush grass to grow, the sort with long and fat blades we made reed whistles out of when we were children on school outings. Back then I didn't know what this type of grass was called. I don't know now, and I will never find out. Between the boulders patches of soft, thick moss darken, which even as an adult I wanted to bed down on. As a child on one of those glorious school trips with our sports teacher and class teacher, we would tumble down the slopes on moss like that, playing games from the cartoon "Gummi Bears" that they used to show on weekends on the only good TV channel. Moss up to our knees. We used it as pillows. Gray boulders, covered in yellowish and salt-and-pepper lichen. A Martian landscape.

"You said we can get reception here?" Zoïa asked, gasping.

I looked around.

"You should already be able to."

She turned on her phone. She walked up and down and in circles with it. No signal. I turned mine on. The same. We walked up the slope. I recalled the signal tower must have been somewhere on this side of the mountain. Lower down in the village the fog had dissipated. The visibility was like a photograph in high resolution: I could see the houses, the barns, the haystacks. No smoke curled from the chimneys. In those conditions I could have distinguished each individual sheep in a flock. But I couldn't see any sheep. No cows. Nor horses. Above the mountains in shades of azure and navy, the sky bore down on us, its concave hemisphere physically visible. On this rounded cover, at an altitude of ten kilometers in the troposphere, hung the claw-like cirrus clouds, painted in translucent strokes.

"Our parents are probably worried," said Zoïa. She was holding her phone above her head and whirling it in different directions like she was hoping to catch a direct satellite signal.

"We said we'd only phone if something happened."

"Well, I'm starting to worry. Besides, I fancy some fresh bread."

"Don't worry. The signal's gone down in Kyiv before—maybe some of the wires were severed when the weather front passed over? Or something on the signal tower got wet and short-circuited? Though, yeah, I'd like some bread, too."

We sat on a boulder with the yellowish and salt-and-pepper lichen. We took out a pack of biscuits instead of bread and had a drink. We had climbed to the top of the cleft and gone down the other side, bypassing our round mountain entirely. The juniper here grew less dense. The grass more so. Short, thick, and unexpectedly soft to the touch. The path barely showed itself, just small pads where we could place our feet. The horizon fell away beneath us, unfolding with every step. We departed the volcanic shale to the side where the cozy Carpathians opened to us once more. The mountaintops were rounded and soft-looking as though one could stroke them like a kitten's head. Here one can breathe deeply. Like when in love. You feel at home, like you're not a person anymore but a harmonious element of this tender planet's ecosystem.

Until you come across some of the trash left behind by some imbeciles. They'd made a pile of it. Burned it on the mountainside. Clearly they'd liked the view and took a stop. Bunch of ignorant jerks. This was why Zoïa and I stopped going to the Chornohora mountain range. What could be their reasoning? Say you're taking a break from the wind in a small niche between the rocks. You look at the navy-blue mountain ridges and ponder: *Could that be Romania I see on the horizon? Am I fantasizing, or do the Romanian mountains seem bluer, as the proverbial grass seems greener on the other side*? As you climb the ridge, you see another tourist who assures you that where you were looking lies the borderlands. You look and look and within you forms an archetype of weird and wondrous lands, places you cannot reach without trials and tribulations. Where dragons dwell. You sit and fantasize, not so much about Romania (where you've actually been and you know it's not that wondrous at all) but about dragons, the Middle Ages, the rings of the Nibelungen, or hobbits or whatever else you're interested in. And then you rummage in your rucksack. *Ooh! I forgot about the treats left in there, let's lighten the load of this rucksack,* and you think, *Oh, I needn't carry this oily can all the way down. I'll leave it here on the ground and just shit all over the fairy-tale*. Why? What are you thinking? "The water washes it all away," eh?

Zoïa silently cleaned up the pile of discarded biscuit wafer wrappers and cigarette packets and put them in a plastic bag in my rucksack. I stopped. I had stripped down to the waist an hour before and was sweating intensely. I only experienced this pleasant feeling of being both scorched by the sun and cooled by the wind at the same time in the mountains. Even the rubbing of the straps on my shoulders was pleasurable. Though maybe that's just an unexplored kink. I took off one strap and carried the bag on one shoulder. The wind dried my wet back. Of course, when I realized that I was sunburned, it was already too late. I put my T-shirt back on, but the straps still rubbed through it. Mercilessly. Oh well. Still satisfying in its own way.

We reached the peak after lunch. The horizon beneath us unfurled out all three hundred and sixty degrees. The village had long disappeared from view. We could only see the mountains. The wind blew freely. It felt as though there was no one around for dozens, or even hundreds of miles.

Indeed, by then that was the case.

6

When the sunburn on my shoulders and my chest started peeling some days later, the pleasurable sensation still had not left me. I lay on my stomach, back of my hand beneath my cheek. Zoïa sat astride my back and carefully removed the strips of skin. I heard a muffled *shhh* as she pulled them off. It tickled a little.

But afterwards we had a row. In bed, no less. I was lying there lazily, the sun shone through my squinting eyelids, and she sat naked on top of me, smearing a pleasurably cool cream on my chest. Then she stopped.

"Let's go down to the village."

"M-hm-m."

"Don't just say, 'm-hm-m,' I'm worried."

"M-hm-m."

"What does 'm-hm-m' mean?"

"I already tried."

I turned away from the window and opened my eyes.

"And? You couldn't?"

"Kinda."

And it kind of didn't feel ok to recount in detail—even less so out loud—the physical sensations I experienced at the time. Especially since I hadn't told her straightaway.

It was not the first time we discussed going down the mountain. At first, I just teased her, like, "I don't want to see other people, you're the only one I want." After that, I made two attempts to sneak down the moor and towards the village. I fantasized about bringing her something crunchy, fresh, like cucumbers, and I'd say, "Surprise!" and I'd see the look on her face.

Only I could not force myself down there. Either time.

The first time I got to the upper edge of the forest beneath the moor, to the spot where the road forded our little stream. To the wooden footbridge made of water-blackened logs. I sat on the footbridge and then I decided against going further, I couldn't explain why. I climbed down the slippery rocks down to the brook, drank my fill of cold water and turned back.

The second time, about ten days later, I got ready to leave in the morning. Zoïa was asleep. I often went walking before dawn, returning around evening. Nothing out of habit, only this time I would return bearing gifts from civilization. Or so I thought.

I crossed the stream via the darkened, wet footbridge and didn't stop. Despite the inexplicable anxiety needling me. I started my descent through the forest. The sun peered through the sparse pines and the birds were chattering in song; I was happy and light, feeling myself, feeling like a bit of a hero, and my quest was going well. A sense of bliss, and it was growing. Joy entered me, so intense, to the point where I wanted to lie down right there and dissolve forever, because I knew I would never feel ecstasy like that again in my life. It was similar to that cloud in my stomach after the lovemaking: that same, pleasurable weakness appeared, only now it didn't fade away, on the contrary growing stronger, more solid, welling up in my cells in metastases of pleasure, as my body seemed to dissolve into air. It felt like floating, trembling with pleasure within every point of a deeply three-dimensional, elastically soft, electrified body that was now translucent, enabling an intoxicated self-examination. It was exaltation, feeling as if at this very moment I could happily disappear, or rather, disappear from happiness. I could become part of the great cosmos, my protons and electrons dispersing across the galaxy to become the building blocks of new stars. And so I may joyfully, readily fade out, weather away . . .

Stop. And there I stopped smiling like an idiot. With a focused effort of thought, I regrouped my muscles which seemed separated from me by whole kilometers. I arrived back at myself and stopped dead. The birds sang like never before. They were screaming! I was floating in the ether of their song. The sound of it soaked through me. Total immersion. Dissolution.

I looked at my faraway hands. They were lightly trembling. Now I felt afraid. I had never seen every single hair on my forearm stand on end, right before my eyes. My body tensed like a porcupine, ready to defend its integrity.

The entire surface of my skin was twitching, like that of a horse when a gadfly lands on it. What on earth was this serotonin rush? I pivoted slowly, and tentatively, as if trying to escape a bear that hadn't yet pounced. I climbed the track back uphill, I crossed the footbridge without stopping and came out into the open, all the while trying not to get lost in my own self, to apprehend the external, to capture the wind with my skin while filtering out the ecstasy through force of will and separating physical sensation from the accompanying pleasure, to listen to the unseen birds chitter away without letting this chittering echo rebound in my mind and take me away from myself. *Yes, yes, it's lovely, but those chords are not arching toward the heavens; take away this excess, just feel the uneven track beneath your feet, just restrain the pleasure the balls of your feet receive from the pressure of each footstep. Concentrate.*

The further up I moved, the clearer my head became. Left behind was only the opaque revelation that one can actually die from an excess of pleasure. Which frightens me still. Of course, one day we all must disintegrate and turn into matter for stardust, losing our wholeness and sentience, but it was pretty scary giving myself away so readily.

I tried to recall what we had eaten that day. Obviously, the first thing I thought of was mushrooms. Not recently. Hm. Maybe that bloody tinker Vasyl, moving contraband Polish canned meat, had sprinkled LSD on it. Or maybe I ate too much salo, which is like ecstasy for Ukrainians, after all. God—at least my sense of humor was coming back, although it was even more pathetic than usual. And self-deprecating humor seemed like a particularly healthy sign. The stars will have to wait before they can have my protons.

I then spent the whole day watching Zoïa suspiciously. We had eaten the same food, but Zoïa behaved normally. Calm, a few sarcastic jibes in the background, some fleeting irritation. But no unhealthy glint in her eyes.

7

We probably spent another whole month there on the round-topped mountain. Only now, everything was completely different. I denied that something was wrong, but every time I thought of returning, I started to panic.

"We said we'd sit it out here the whole summer, if we can . . ."

"Even if the world ends?" Zoïa interrupted. "Ok. I can't. I admit it. Happy?"

"Well, even if the world does end, where better to sit it out than here?" I tried to make it sound like a joke, but a tone of irritation rang through my voice, and Zoïa could tell.

"I said that I can't anymore. Did you hear me?"

Zoïa had also tried to sneak down to the village without me knowing. She came back after three hours. Downcast. She only told me the following day. She said she felt drained. That she was not used to walking so far. No, she hadn't felt anything ridiculous in the forest like I had described. She just grew tired and walked back, that's it. It was too far to go to the village on foot. It was a stupid idea. We had to take the car.

To me, firing up Raquel would have been total capitulation. We were both healthy and fine. Why panic? Why cut short our blissful holiday?

Although, there was no more bliss. We were constantly arguing or not talking to each other. We each kept to ourselves. Zoïa would read and not speak. I would bring her tea and she would nod, thanks, without taking her eyes off the book. When the rains came again three days later, I took my raincoat and tried to go out walking like before. Yet instead of meditation and a happy, wet face, I experienced a slow boil inside me; I would return to sit and sulk on the threshold, rather than do the same inside the house. I would sweat under the steaming raincoat as my legs would freeze, and inside me was only irritation, rage, and stubbornness: Nope, I'm staying here, like I planned. Until the end of summer. I won't budge. What, change our plans because of Zoïa's vague cravings, or because Uncle Vasyl was a fat load of help and we were living off nonperishables? Or because we were shocked to discover—again!—that there is no phone reception in the mountains?

"I'm sorry." She came up to me on the threshold. "Sometimes I get carried away."

She sat next to me and she leaned her head on my shoulder. I melted. She was making peace even though I was the one in the wrong. For this, I adored Zoïa.

"I get it. You were getting yourself wound up." *Why am I saying this*, I think, *why am I putting this on her again*? I continued, "Shall we drive down in a week if Vasyl doesn't come by?"

She nodded and lifted her head off my shoulder. I turned to look at her. She had shut her eyes. I thought she was doing it for show and I got angry again. Too little time to calm down properly: a mix of cortisol and adrenaline was still pumping through my bloodstream. Or whatever it was. But I didn't want to argue again. Not until she whispered, tragically: "I thought you would offer to go today."

"Why didn't you say so?!"

"Whatever. You sit here. Enjoy your solitude."

With that possessive word, she emphatically excluded herself from "my" solitude.

Well. In that case, I'm out.

I got up and went into the house. I grabbed a jacket and raincoat, took some baked potatoes wrapped in foil out of the oven, put them straight in my pocket, zipped up my coat, and walked out.

"I'm going for a walk," I muttered to Zoïa, not touching her. I went around the hut and started scrambling up the mountain. I needed to tire myself out. In a big way.

I walked down again late that evening. Wisps of white fog descended onto the navy blue twilight. From below, the crawling fog must have looked like clouds clinging to the mountain. The slender silhouette of a young spruce sliced this shroud into pieces. I stood spellbound and watched how the white ribbon of fog crept downwards, flowing around the tree, how it gently fell apart and then thickened once again ten meters past the tree trunk. The gap in this milky stream made me think of a dark spindle. I turned off the path and walked straight up to the spruce, to the center of this spindle. I ran my hand along the moist, coarse trunk. I sat with my back to it and felt the knotted bark through my coat. The grass was the same species unknown to me since childhood, with the tubular, slim blades that provided almost no surface for water to collect on them. My grass seat was almost dry. The spruce needles wove a cocoon of silence above me. There was no wind. So how then, I wondered, were the wisps of fog moving? Just the change in air pressure? Or temperature? Why was my understanding of the Earth so bad? Why was I so angry at Zoïa?

From beneath the tree, I could see the shroud of fog was evenly dense. Its passage imperceptible. To see it you had to be outside of it. It was like the passage of history, at least when no wars or revolutions are happening. Once you step away, look around, you understand how much has happened and changed while you were inside of it. If you were to step out and look at me from the path, I might have struck a quite romantic figure: a man sitting against a tree trunk, hugging his knees, melancholically gazing into the mist.

Only, by then, there would have been no one left to look at this figure.

I returned to the hut after dark and quietly entered the bedroom. Zoïa was gone. Fear suddenly clutched my throat, like the sure hand of a sadist surgeon pulling your gullet inside out. I tried to swallow or breathe, but I could not. My whole body convulsively twitched to the soles of my feet. I grabbed my neck, below the ears, and I swiped my palm forcibly downwards. It seemed to help a little and I inhaled. Now something caught at my chest: I rubbed at my sternum, but I could not rub away the invisible lump that was there.

Had someone been here? Zoïa was alone, a woman in the forest, and I wasn't there for her. She might have screamed. I was on the other side of the mountain, and I didn't hear. Mushroom pickers? Poachers? Drunken men? Or the bears that Vasyl was talking about? A lynx? They say lynxes are scarier than bears. Less predictable.

No. I know what could be worse than lynxes.

Back when I used to help my grandfather drive his herd in the village, the storks would walk among the cattle, but they would not let me near. I asked my grandfather why storks were not afraid of cows but were of me, even though I was ten times smaller than a cow.

"Because cows are animals," my grandfather answered. "But man is a beast."

I took a flashlight. We had barely used it yet. I circled the house. Sharp shadows shot up with every movement. No signs anywhere. There was a dishwashing sponge on the path. We had been looking for it during the day. It must have fallen there.

Zoïa left me! I sprang to Raquel. I couldn't open the car because

I'd forgotten in my panic that it was locked. I rushed up to the house with the flashlight, the shadows springing at me. I almost fell over the threshold and dove toward the inner flap of my rucksack for the keys.

For a while the car wouldn't start. Please don't let the battery be dead, please, please . . . Yes, it's started, thank you, dear Raquel, don't let me down. I sat behind the wheel and tried not to shake, counting the seconds, giving the car time to warm up so it wouldn't stall straightaway. Two minutes would make no difference. But ninety seconds should be enough, eh, Raquel, old girl? The aged CD player finally decided to load itself and with a creak put on the next disk, and out tumbled the bourbon-soaked, tarmac-smashed, run-over-by-a-truck voice of Tom Waits. I shuddered and turned down the sound. "Nice and smooth, nice and smooth," I told myself out loud, though my wish was not fulfilled. I turned on the headlights. Vertical tree trunks leapt out in the darkness. The headlights penetrated deep through the forest. I noticed something small scurry off to one side. I lowered the windows on both sides and slowly reversed: There was no place to turn around until we got back to the road. Why hadn't I backed in? We learned this in training classes after the war started in the East. Why, why? *Come on. Don't rush.* I tried to keep control over my panic: *Slowly, slowly, I must go slowly, I cannot stall, can't drive into a boulder.* The back of my seat was already soaked with my sweat. *Don't stall, you don't know how much battery is left. Why didn't we take off the battery terminals? I don't know how many more times we can turn on the engine, just don't stall.* I slowly crawled out of our hollow, what was I thinking when I parked? *Slowly now. Right, that's it.* I turned Raquel around and drove along the creased grass. I remembered that the road sometimes curved around the boulders. There, the first one approached: moist and covered in a yellow-gray lichen. I maneuvered around it.

I heard the engine, my breathing, and a quiet hissing in the player: the disc was still spinning. I turned the sound up a bit, counting on Waits's meditative power, jabbing the forward button a few times, searching for a more calming melody. "Charlie, I'm pregnant and living on 9th Street . . ." I rubbed my eyes with my fist. The two of us, Zoïa and I, had never been pregnant, and now it would never happen. Maybe it was nothing serious and all we needed was some help from modern medicine, but we'd been waiting: We'll go see a doctor after we get an apartment, we said; we're not in a rush, we said. So we stopped using protection: Whatever happens, happens. But now it wouldn't happen. I uttered a sob.

I entered the village half an hour later. It was pitch black. There were no lights on anywhere. Not a single lamp in the whole village. I drove to Uncle Vasyl's, left Raquel with the engine running in front of the locked gates, climbed over them and peered into the windowpanes. No, if Zoïa were here they wouldn't be sleeping. Maybe.

A merciless stench came from somewhere.

I climbed back over and drove to the lowest part of the village and made a U-turn at the crossroads by the church. No lights were on anywhere. At least the dogs weren't howling the whole village down, like they love to do. No. Zoïa wouldn't go to people she didn't know, that would be out of character. Especially in the middle of the night. She was somewhere on the mountain. Maybe she had fallen. Broken her leg. I drove back.

Driving back out of the village, I could no longer restrain myself and started hitting the car horn. Maybe Zoïa was lost? I beeped more, and longer, until it was almost continuous, I accelerated and nearly ran into the lichen-covered rock from earlier. I braked, my bumper ending up a few centimeters away from the slippery, wet surface of the rock. I pressed the horn and held it. A long wail.

I had to reverse to maneuver past the rock. I could no longer shake off the panic, I was shaking and I knew that in that state I would never be able to get into the recess beside the house, not front first and certainly not by backing in, so I stopped the car on the track, slammed the doors and ran down the slope, accidentally banging my big toe against the wall, I ran into the hut, and there was Zoïa, sitting on the bed.

"Why are you honking down the whole mountain?"

"Where. Have. You. Been?!"

"Let go. Let go!"

I had grabbed her shoulders and was shaking her. Gently, I imagined, but her head was actually being thrown back and forth.

"Zoïa. Where were you?"

"Where were you?"

"Looking for you."

"And I was looking for you. You just left! I walked to the village. There was nothing there. What was it you were going on about? 'Impossible, evil, taboo, death.' You made it all up! Why the hell did you do that?"

"Zoïa. Zoïa."

By the time we had calmed down, dawn was moving in.

We had missed each other. To be fair, Zoïa had lost her way in the dark for a short while, taking the wrong road out of the village. She arrived on an unknown moor, got scared in the dark, realized her mistake, found the right way and returned to the house, when she saw the car was gone. So she sat on the bed, wrapped in a blanket, and then listened to the approach of Raquel and her horn.

"Zoïa, did you see anyone in the village? Anyone at all?"

"It was nighttime, everyone was sleeping."

I sat by the bed until Zoïa fell asleep. Outside was already quite gray. A rainy sky hung overhead. My temple throbbed. I was never a big drinker, but I felt now was the time for that vodka. I sat on the porch and stared dumbly at the broken zig-zag that divided the navy forest and gray sky, sipping at an enamel cup to create some fire in my throat.

Zoïa slept restlessly. She thrashed and turned in her sleep. She got up to go to the toilet and as she walked past me to go outside. She caught sight of the bottle.

"Seriously?"

I silently went to bed. Later I awoke and it was still just as gray. A sickening rain lightly pattered on the windowsill. My eyes hurt. I turned onto my back and knew straightaway a headache was coming. It was not as bad if I lay on my side.

Outside, the round-topped mountain hung over us. I found it painful to look at the massif. If I tried to look at it obliquely, my eyeballs hurt from inside. I stared like a dope at the bedside wall that had been rubbed by the passage of many bodies. I ran my finger over it. Higher up by the windowsill, the whitewash was pleasantly coarse but opposite me, where for years backs had been brushing against the wall, the white lime had turned into a gray, polished surface, repellent to the touch.

Where was Zoïa?

I turned onto my other side, frowning from the pain between my brows. Zoïa sat on the chair, back towards me. I knew she could hear me creaking the bedsprings. She was reading, or pretending to.

"What time is it?"

"Two p.m."

I yawned and turned onto my back, and when the pain that had been running in waves over my head passed a little, I gently turned my head so I would not look obliquely at the mountain, but straight at it. The round peak was visible through the foul drizzle, darkening against the light gray backdrop. The mountain. Our savior.

8

The downpour that began that evening was not prepared to stop. Huge drops blown up into bubbles fell into the puddle beneath Raquel's wheels from trees unable to support any more moisture. Vertical gray stripes covered the mountain, which seemed to float in the distance. We waited for a day under this constant rattling and barely spoke to one another.

We could not wait any longer. That morning, when Zoïa and I were leaving, the downpour intensified once more. I wanted to go stand in the hollow and look upon the mountain that had saved us (this I already understood), but Zoïa sat like a mannequin in the car, and I was scared that our mutual irritation would develop into another fight.

Raquel's windscreen wipers could not work fast enough, the water enveloped us. I turned on the music. Waits' voice matched my mental state. At the line, ". . . you got me checkin' in my rearview mirror," I tried to look in Raquel's mirror for the mountain, but of course you can't check out a whole mountain in a rearview mirror.

The car sloshed along the waterlogged road. I was afraid we'd get stuck. True, there were no big puddles or potholes, only the rusty red mud and scattered piles of fine, sharp pebbles. Fortunately, the ground here was rocky, which tends to slow erosion.

Stop. I feel like I've expressed the exact same thought, before, in the exact same words—is that true? I don't know.

The village stood empty. The downpour enveloped us. We drove up to Vasyl's. I jumped over the fence again. The house was locked. I knocked. I tugged the handle and felt a rough crustiness against my palm: the door handle had rusted.

I put the keys to our alpine hut into a Nescafe tin on the windowsill, first pouring out Vasyl's soggy cigarette butts straight onto the grass. I stood on the veranda and took out my phone to call Vasyl and tell him where the keys were and to arrange payment to his bank account, since he wasn't home. But there was no mobile phone signal.

Apart from the noise of the rainfall there was no sound anywhere. Not a single cow lowing or a pig grunting. Then, I finally knew something was wrong. This was the second time I had broken into the yard and the dog had not come after me. I turned to the kennel. The chain led inside it. What was it called? I couldn't remember. A massive white body could be seen deep inside the kennel. I slowly approached it, whistling like how you whistle at dogs, preparing to jump back.

"Here doggy . . . Goood boy . . ."

I leaned towards it and saw white teeth, bared. I stumbled and fell onto my hands in the mud. The dog's lips had been eaten away by white worms, maggots crawled on its jaws, its dirty body was sunken under the thick white fur. Its eyes were also gone. And only now, up close, the stench of dead flesh, the same I smelled the previous time, but had not recognized.

Zoïa whacked open the doors once she saw me on my hands and knees in the wet mud. I feebly gestured at her not to come closer. I couldn't tell her, I was pushing back down what was rising up inside of me. I stood up and took a breath, coughed gingerly to clear my throat, walked away and stood back against the fence, raising my face towards the oncoming rain.

"You look like you have jaundice," said Zoïa.

"Please. Not now."

I splashed some cold water on my chest. I felt a little better. Zoïa stood next to me without speaking, and once I felt better, I realized my gratitude for her presence.

"Do you think that Vasyl and his wife are inside the house?"

"I'm not going inside. We should call someone."

We went back to the car and drove down into the village. There was no one anywhere. The gates to Vasyl's cousin's house, the one who kept the sawmill, were open. I got out of the car and went into his yard. I pulled the doorknob and the house opened.

"Praise Jesus! Is anyone in?"

My voice sounded shrill. Standing on the veranda, I looked back to the car. Zoïa got out to be with me, and I realized then how much I loved her.

"What is it?" she asked.

I shivered, wet all over.

"Hello!" Zoïa called into the house.

We listened. I held my breath, but the sound of my heartbeat was too loud. The rain was striking the tin roof above. After a few seconds I couldn't hold it in and my loud breathing even drowned out the sound of the rain.

"We should go in," Zoïa said.

I looked around, went out into the rain and tried to tear a post from the little gate. The top broke off in my hand. The wood was slimy and foul. I threw away the piece and pulled off another slat from the center. There was a screech of a nail. The plank came off the upper crossbar. I bent the slat towards the ground and gave it a few sharp kicks to release it from the bottom of the post. A long, bent nail was left sticking out of the plank. All the better. I clutched the half-rotten plank, not raising it, so I wouldn't look any more pathetic than I already did, and dragged it along.

Zoïa didn't say a word.

We entered the little house. It smelled of dry dust, sacks of grain. The house was clean and empty. Except for the mouse droppings on the kitchen table.

9

The shop, the village council, and the post office were all locked. We returned to Vasyl's yard, where I took a hoe from the shed and broke the window with its long handle.

Inside, there were no signs of struggle or a quick exit. A loaf of bread bloomed with mold on the sideboard. A dry, mummified mouse lay in the corner. Scattered over the floor and furniture were tiny pieces of evidence attesting that the mice now considered the house their own.

I forced myself to go into the barn despite the reek. I had to know. No, no people were inside. The cow, horse, and pigs locked inside that could not get out when the people disappeared had already long starved to death, like the dog.

Overko. I only then remembered it, clutching at the memory of his name instead of the memory of what he looked like now.

"Let's get away from here."

"Wait," said Zoïa.

She went into the shed where I had found the hoe. She came back with an axe and put it in the footwell of the car. I felt a weakness in my legs and stomach. Like I was gradually disappearing. Dissolving.

As we started up Raquel, I noticed a chicken in the wet bush. A live one.

"She's sheltering from the rain."

"Good for her. She managed to get out."

"The people might have, too. Maybe they left."

Zoïa did not reply to this. We set off.

Beyond the village, a small herd of cows were getting drenched in the rain. Seven or so. They were clearly the ones that were outside when this happened.

Whatever it was that happened.

I stopped Raquel and walked over to the cows: the first large living creatures I had seen yet. But they shied away from me. Normal cows don't do that. Normally, it's you who have to step back for them. Or stop your car to let the herd pass. These ones retreated, side-eyeing me. The cows' udders were painfully overfull. I then noticed a bull among them. I froze, expecting him to charge. But all he did was low softly, shake his horns, and shuffle away through the bushes to lead the heifers away from me. The cows stepped over a ditch before plunging into a thicket. Their udders slapped heavily against their hind legs. Poor animals. One of them, clearly sick, couldn't cross the ditch. She got stuck and pitched onto her side. She lowed pitifully. I walked up to her, as she thrashed about and swung her head.

Zoïa got out the car.

"Look how swollen she is."

The cow lay uncomfortably on her side. Milk oozed from her udder, although this was not what tortured the animal. Her stomach was terribly distended. Maybe the wet grass had started fermenting inside her, I don't know. I heard once that emergency vets pierce animals' stomachs with special pointed tubes to let the gases out, but what could we do? I thought about the axe that would end this cow's suffering, but I knew I couldn't do it. The feeling of weakness grew stronger. The rain almost stopped.

We drove further and further down and we saw no people. I was afraid that sooner or later I would start seeing dead bodies, but there were no bodies either. In one large village several dogs rushed out to our car. Small ones. The kind of dogs that village people don't chain. The downpour started hammering down again and this, alongside the sight of living dogs, made us feel a little better.

Toward evening we drove into the little town where I grew up. I steered Raquel into the yard of my old building. The cobbles on the old road roared under the tires. We stopped under the same old willow from which I once fell onto our neighbor's Zhiguli. My insides had hurt for a few days afterwards, but I didn't tell my parents because I was more scared of getting in trouble for the car's bent roof than anything else. Good that there weren't car alarms back then. I was never found out.

I took the axe out of Raquel's footwell.

During that afternoon as I drove, Zoïa tried to phone people, but the connection never came through. Even here, in the town.

I rang the bell upstairs. It didn't work. Somewhere below us a cat mewed loudly and plaintively.

"Mo-om!"

I pounded my fist on the door, pounded so hard I was wheezing.

Zoïa then started breaking down the door with the axe. The doors were old, oak, made back when we were ruled by Poland before WWII. Zoïa quickly ran out of breath, so I hacked and hacked, often missing, at the boards, and I was hyperventilating by the time we entered the flat. Mom's laptop was on the table. In sleep mode. That battery really lasts. It looked like there had been no electricity for a long time. Her open tabs included Gmail and a knitting site with a pattern of cornflowers. Zoïa always joked that they were her "spirit" flowers. So, Mom was making something for Zoïa when this all happened. Round needles, a ball of yarn, and her unfinished piece lay to the side. It didn't look like Mom had left in a hurry. There was no note. She knew we were in the Carpathians, and that we would stop by for a few days on our way back.

I went through both rooms. Not a single sign of hurry or panic. When I opened the fridge in the kitchen, rancid water leaked out from under the sealing rubber. I winced and closed the door.

Knowing my mother, if there was even a one in ten chance of being among the saved, she would not only find a way to survive but also save others. If there had been any chance.

I wanted to disappear, I just wanted to disappear. To fade out, weather away and cease to exist.

10

We pushed silently eastward, having joined the Kyiv-Chop highway after driving a hundred kilometers through potholed, semi-tarmacked or dirt roads. The night started to grow blue. Soon it would be dawn. While the pouring rain wove its cocoon around us, things were bearable. No thoughts. You just keep spinning the wheels through the downpour, between potholes filled with muddy water. When we came out of the weather front while on the highway, an old yellow moon crept out and soared above us between torn shreds of cloud. The moon had two or three days left to live. I envied him. I also desired to wane just as imperceptibly, melt away, only now this desire was a somber one, not at all like in the forest. I also had a wild desire for sex, so much so my hands shook. Zoïa, the same. We stopped on the hard shoulder and did it quickly and joylessly. An urgent, animal compulsion, an attempt to preserve the species, a biological function spared of emotional intimacy. And we didn't worry someone would catch us doing it.

"Let's keep driving. I'm done," Zoïa said straight afterwards.

She already felt it. As soon as we had come out of the rain, the same physical sensation came over her too. Empty-headedness, a weakened heart, insides coldly putrefying. Flexible limbs, boneless rubber. Muscles atrophying, the weakening skeleton, the softening mind—all painlessly, which is the most frightening part of it: dissolving imperceptibly into your surroundings, slowly filing down like the moon, and then becoming translucent, and you weather away into thin air. And you wish for it. The weathering. Like volcanic rocks on the side of the mountain. A washed away road. Strange rock formations in Utah and Arizona. The weathering pleasantly empties you of consciousness, but your instincts rise up against it, forcing your hairs to stand on end, forcing you to shake yourself out like a dog that has just got out of the water and, instead of lying down and accepting dissolution into gentle nonexistence—*Rage against it, flee*!

But your instincts don't tell you where to flee. A memory informed by an ancient, probably inherited habit, tells us to always flee westward. At the start of the war, I got drunk with a schoolmate (to whose children I was godfather—he had already had two by then), and we discussed where we would run to if anything ever happened. We decided that the mountain border between Ukraine and Romania was the least monitored, so if anything happened, that would be the best place to bribe either their or our border guards and sneak through. This memory now seemed so funny that I wanted to stop the car and just laugh it all out, bent double and holding my stomach. My diaphragm spasmed, and I grew scared: *It's hysteria*. We just had to push on and not think. Zoïa said we should go to her parents. They lived on the other side of the Dnipro river. Go via Kyiv, spend the night at our place on Rusanivka island, and carry on. If we don't weather away in our sleep. Ever since the rain stopped, this weathering feeling increased dramatically. The water that "washes everything away" had disappeared.

We had to push on. We moved along the highway eastward.

"I want to have sex again," said Zoïa in a hoarsened voice.

She actually used the ruder verb, uncharacteristically for her. Perhaps five hours had passed since the previous time. Like the weathering, our sensations were synchronized: my desire had wildly increased, too, I'd just kept quiet out of fear that it was inappropriate.

"I thought it was just me."

"Stop. Right here," she said with a hoarse and half-hysterical laugh.

This time was even more frantic. Even more joyless. But at least we had the urge to fight for our lives.

"How long have we been together and never tried it in the car? And now, twice in a day," said Zoïa, pulling on her jeans.

"It's a bit cramped."

"Who said it would be easy?"

The sun rose in an already clear sky and now shone in my eyes as well as reflected off the wet road. A cleansed morning of blistering beauty. As if nothing had happened. Cats scurried about in the villages, chickens walked beside the fences. A great clamor of rooks soared over the field.

"I'm starting to think the Earth just got sick of us and rid itself of humans," Zoïa spoke up, looking straight ahead and not at me. "Well, that's if I thought the planet was sentient. You remember the old skits about how we arrogantly think that we are the crowning glory of creation, but actually the biosphere just needs plastic and that was our real function? We've fulfilled that function, so now we're made for the junkyard.

"Or maybe we were designed to dig more carbon from the ground, so the plants could grow better. Or humans are just fertilizer, but you know the sort that scorches the earth when there's too much of it. So now the planet is shuffling us off this mortal coil on our behalf—and nicely, too. Like euthanasia. Have you noticed how easy and painless it is, dissolving?"

"Weathering," I corrected her, teeth clenched, not tearing my gaze from the road.

"What's that? But jeez, it's so harsh! Maybe the fertilizer wants to live, too!"

"Calm down," I said, straining to speak.

"No wait, listen! I prefer to think that we did it to ourselves. Nuclear weapons, or an artificial virus, the American biolabs, terrorism, war, China, Russia, North Korea. It's somehow easier knowing that we did this to ourselves, rather than . . . being destined to become manure to fertilize this planet. Or hey, I guess some super-super-super-phosphate fertilizer, if we wanted to preserve our own sense of self-importance. A superphosphate that accidentally became conscious, not to mention self-reproducing. About self-reproduction, by the way—I think I'll feel like it again soon."

Zoïa pressed her lips tight.

It was a long time since she had talked so much. So far, Zoïa was holding out well, better than I was. But sooner or later the crisis would have to come.

Something inside the car snapped, and it lost traction. Raquel wheeled on by momentum, bit by bit losing speed.

I leaned under the wheel and poked at the switch.

"Again?"

"No. We just ran out of gas."

"What region are we in right now?"

"Rivne . . . The land of storks."

"Huh?"

"Never mind. A memory."

It was somewhere here, twenty kilometers from this highway, where I used to spend every summer as a child, where my grandfather and I would herd cows, where every other telephone pole in the village had a stork's nest on top of it. The people never bothered the storks, but the birds nonetheless never let people near them. They rattled their beaks and, settling their heads on their backs, they hatched chicks, and perhaps their little brains even understood that we humans were protecting their nests from predators by our presence, but they still kept us at a distance; calmly hunting frogs amongst the cows on the water meadows, they would shuffle sideways away from us cowherds, from me. Because cows are animals, but man is a beast.

We stopped at Velyka Omeliana, at the gas station. I wheeled Raquel over to the gas pump. On trips abroad I had learned how to pump the gas myself, since gas station workers are not as common there. No gas came out. I didn't know exactly how much we had in the tank.

"It's ok. We have enough."

"For what?" Zoïa giggled nervously.

"To get to Kyiv."

She did not ask, "Why Kyiv?" And I was grateful for that. The sliding doors at the gas station were also not working. I took a red fireman's axe with a long iron handle out of the sand tub in the extinguisher stand and, with surprising ease, in one strike I smashed half of the glass doors. The glass shattered.

An alarm. A sharp, unpleasant noise that cut to the bone. The tone was clearly selected with prior thought, to be as noxious as possible. Only now, no one will come when it starts screeching.

The two of us, Zoïa and I, loitered about the shelves and fridges. Any real food had long gone bad. We grabbed some packets of crisps and Snickers and piled them on the back seat. We filled the trunk with bottled water. There was no coffee. I drank as much cola as I could, hoping for a caffeine rush. It did not help; I was drifting off. I was afraid of falling asleep and never waking up.

"Let me drive," said Zoïa.

She had a driver's license. She got more lessons with a private instructor after she passed her test, but she never learned to love driving. She sat behind the wheel, and I sat next to her.

"Keep an eye on me, please," I asked. "I don't want to, you know. Disappear."

I tipped back the passenger's seat and felt that I really wanted to. Disappear. My body wanted it. I passed out.

I woke up from the feeling the car had stopped. I looked around, and Zoïa was no longer beside me.

11

I scrabbled to get up, but the seatbelt snapped me back.

It took me a few tries to unclip myself because I could not steady my fingers to hit the clasp, by which time my lips were trembling too.

I got out of the car ready to scream but stopped myself.

She was a hundred meters from the car. In a field. She was hunched over on one knee. I ran over to her, tripping over beetroot leaves. She heard my footsteps, or my breathing, placidly turned her head and held out her palm towards me. I slowed to a walk and approached, my throat dried out.

"I almost . . ."

"*Shhh.*"

I wanted to clear my throat, but before this, she said in a low whisper: "Look."

Her body had been hiding the stork from view. The bird was shaking and twitching. He turned his head to the side and looked at me with one eye. The stork looked dirty and ill.

"Zoïa, jeez, I nearly died . . ."

"Me too."

"I mean, I woke up and you weren't there, I thought I . . ."

At that, a sob. It was from the shame that I nearly blurted, "I thought I was left alone," instead of saying, "I thought you'd disappeared."

"He was just standing on the side of the road."

"Who?"

"The pig wearing lipstick. The stork, you twit."

"Oh. Why did you walk so far away?"

"He ran off."

"Because man is a beast," I blurted out absentmindedly.

"That's exactly what I thought. Look. He has a broken leg. He tried to fly away, but he couldn't take off from the one leg."

We christened the stork "Bousko," like they call storks out in the country, and we took him with us. Zoïa found a few sticks, took out a roll of bandages from the first aid kit, and made me squeeze Bousko's wings tightly under my arm and hold his beak; I turned away, and Zoïa cold-bloodedly set his bones. I don't know if she did it right. But after the war started, everyone at her organization was sent to first aid courses. I felt the stork shudder in my arms and maybe, if he could, he would have shrieked. I imagined how I might react to someone setting my bones without anesthesia.

Zoïa and Bousko sat in the back seat, and we set off. She is one of those people who has a special sensitivity to the suffering of animals. And I am probably one of those for whom people are more important, even at the expense of other species. She once called this "speciesism." In jest—or maybe not.

Sitting in the back, Bousko nodded his head on his long neck, trying to keep it steady despite the movement of the car. I looked at him and Zoïa in the rearview mirror and after experiencing that fear of loss, I suddenly acknowledged how we had been together for so many years, but I had never truly understood how precious she was to me, even more than my own mother. At the thought of my mother, tears came to my eyes—but I had to keep going, we had to get to Kyiv, even if I didn't know why, it didn't matter. We just had to move towards a goal.

I thought of how Zoïa would poke fun at old Hollywood films because, she said, they always had to have a happy end, even after nuclear fallout. What would be our happy end? Get to the Paton Bridge in Kyiv and from there toss ourselves into the water? A twenty-meter drop and another ten under the surface. Do we take the stork with us or let him go? Is that speciesism or not? Bousko threw his head back and started clicking his beak.

We did make it to the Paton Bridge, to the beginning of the rise onto the overpass, where the last whiffs of gas evaporated. Raquel barely survived the whole of Kyiv's empty Right Bank, and on every hill I expected her to stop. Running out of gas didn't change anything. We could now reach our flat in Rusanivka on foot.

To do what, though?

Raquel slowly wheeled backwards. I parked her over the Dnipro.

"There we are."

I turned on the car's hazard lights. Automatic reflex. I turned them off. We stood in the middle lane on the wide, empty bridge. Normally, this time of morning would be the end of rush hour, every lane gridlocked with traffic.

Zoïa got out with Bousko under her arm and let him out on the tarmac. The stork hobbled away, unfurling his wings. That was it, time for him to fly away. But Bousko could not. Instead, he stretched, then started smoothing some crumpled feathers with his beak, keeping a few meters' distance from us. I walked over all the empty road lanes towards Rusanivka.

I stopped, and after a few seconds I felt awaken in me, instead of thoughts of being joyfully coaxed to suicide, an animal joy of being alive. The black waves beneath me did not pull me in any longer; on the contrary, they were sucking the blackness out of me.

"The weathering has stopped!"

"Yeah!" Zoïa answered with a shout from the other side of the road. There was also laughter in her voice.

A pleasant wind blew, and it did not threaten to weather me away to nothing. It was refreshing on my face. Concave black ripples roved over the surface of the Dnipro.

"The water washes it all away!" I shouted in glee.

But there I stopped, scared: this all started to remind me of my first serotonin rush, when I walked down the forest in a waterfall of bird sounds and flashes of light, drowned by waves of smells and warmth. No. This was the opposite chemical wave. The feeling that I had stopped weathering away. I was sure.

"Do you think it's the water?" asked Zoïa. She had gone quiet. She had come up to me.

"I don't know. Yes."

It was like the currents that were changing my body chemistry had dispersed: I then remembered the streaks of mist that floated around the pine tree and became invisible when I sat beneath it by the pine trunk. Maybe this unknown something, whatever it is, floats in or is washed away by water. And since she and I, Zoïa and me, had survived, it must surely bypass mountaintops, like the low-lying mist that leaves the peak under the sun. But who would investigate that now?

"Let's go and catch Bousko."

"Look—is it just me, or is that smoke rising over Hydropark?

"It's water vapor, I guess. The sunrise."

The abandoned high-rise hotel that towered over this side of our island neighborhood also seemed to give off smoke. But between us and Rusanivka, in the middle of the river that bisects Kyiv city, lay the tip of Hydropark—well, properly Venetian Island, but people never used that name—and it was unclear whether smoke emerged from it or if the Dnipro flowing between the islands was emitting water vapor.

We left the car where it was, on the rise to the bridge. I stuffed a big hiking rucksack with the bottles of drinking water and Snickers that Zoïa and I had plundered from the gas station. Zoïa took Bousko under her arm.

I was already panting and sweating under the heavy rucksack before we had reached the point where the bridge crossed the bottom tip of Hydropark's island, opening up to a full view of Rusanivka. The smoke was now gone.

"You're right. It was steam."

"So what's that?" Zoïa pointed.

There was no smoke above Rusanivka, now fully visible from the top of the bridge's arch. However, deep inside Hydropark, the other island, several distinct clouds of smoke simultaneously spiraled skywards from beneath the trees along the shoreline.

We walked high over the tip of Hydropark. There were no steps down to the island from the bridge, and we continued on, descending to our own, built-up isle. By now the rucksack was driving me down the slope. I used my knees to brake. We turned onto a smaller bridge over the Rusanivka canal. The high-rise, unfinished Slavutych Hotel took up half the sky before us. We were approaching the coniferous hedge on the edge of the island when two men with Kalashnikovs jumped up from behind it, one pointing his barrel at us and, with horror in his voice, he screamed: "Stop the fuck right there!"

ISLAND

1

"Hands behind your head! On your knees! On your fuckin' knees! Hands behind your heads! The girl as well!"

This must be karma. Even after the end of the world, I still get into these kinds of situations. Heavy rucksack still on, I thumped down onto my knees. Because in these moments there is no question of not obeying: In war or apocalypse, we separate into friends and foes. When you are a civilian, kneeling on the ground with your hands behind your head, the people holding weapons are always your foes.

This time I didn't even get scared. Zoïa was more frightened than I was: she didn't go through this back when the war started. The heavy rucksack put so much pressure on my knees that I silently sat up on my heels. The men did not react to this. Panic flickered in the eyes of the twitchy guy, the one who shouted. It was like he thought Zoïa and I were some sort of zombies, nonhuman. Judging by his behavior, the twitchy guy was clearly subordinate to the other one. At the signal of his superior, he lowered his weapon. I knew that if one of them was going to shoot us, it would have been Mr. Twitch. His ruddy skin clung to his skull, and his bone structure was prominent, kind of like the speed-fiends I know. He shifted his weight from one foot to the other and snorted his nostrils that were thin to the point of transparency.

The senior of the two was a thickset man of about fifty or sixty years of age, your typical Slavic uncle with a beer gut. He looked at us with suspicion, although a glint of laughter ran through his eyes, a readiness, even now, to turn everything into a joke.

"True handchicks?"

"S-sorry?"

"I'm asking, are you true-hands?"

An awkward silence fell.

"We don't understand you," Zoïa said.

"Shit," the twitchy guy twitched.

"Calm down," his senior brought him to heel. "Where've you come here from? And what the hell is that fucking thing?"

"It's not a fucking thing, it's a stork." Zoïa dropped her hands to grab Bousko, but he hopped away, balancing on his good leg. "He joined us on the way."

"On the way from where?"

"The mountains. We were on holiday in the Carpathians."

The twitchy guy huffed and started blabbering something in Russian. His superior once again cut him off with a hand signal.

"Holiday. Mountains. How come you didn't get washed away?"

"Are you talking about the weathering?"

"Same shit, different name," said the hefty guy, now quite good-naturedly. "So, it didn't just miss all the islands? The mountains as well?"

The twitchy one pointed his barrel in our direction, though without raising his weapon, and wailed in a high, wavering voice:

"Uncle Siroja, they're true-hands! There's nothing to discuss with them!"

"Can we get up already?" seethed Zoïa.

Uncle Siroja looked at her in surprise and gestured the *OK*. The twitchy guy clearly didn't like this. But he kept quiet. Uncle Siroja continued to address me, although it was Zoïa who answered mostly. He asked again to make sure we were not true hands, and when Zoïa repeated that we did not even know what he meant, he just nodded westwards, in the direction of Hydropark. He started interrogating us about how we had traveled here from the Carpathian Mountains. Where was our car? Did we know that people were left on Rusanivka after the "washout"? No, we did not. Why had we come? To go to our flat. Or maybe carry on. Hard to explain. Oh, hard, and why's that?

For Uncle Siroja it was just as much a surprise that someone had survived beyond these islands as it was for us to find out that people had survived here. Since it had happened, we were the first to come from the outside. No wonder Mr. Twitch panicked. They asked for our passports to prove that we lived on Rusanivka. This did not help at all. Being migrants to the city, our documents were not registered with a Kyiv address.

"We have a key!" Zoïa appealed to them.

"A key, yes, but no registration . . ."

"Boss!" I exclaimed, and instantly felt ashamed about using that word. "This is Kyiv, half the people here aren't registered."

Mr. Twitch shot a hate-filled glance at me.

"Well, well, what am I to do with you two, then?" Uncle Siroja drawled.

His silky tone told me we could settle this. This intonation, peculiar to traffic cops, bureaucrats, and housing department functionaries, was known to me since childhood. Of course. Why would something like, you know, the end of the world change people? Uncle Siroja slapped his thigh with our passports.

"Alrighty. Why don't we find a solution to this, eh?"

Uncle Siroja left Mr. Twitch at the checkpoint by the empty hotel, and went with us himself to, I quote, check the key fit. We walked down the riverfront past the statue of Gogol. Uncle Siroja whistled with satisfaction and drummed his fingers on the butt of his AK. He was relaxed. Zoïa carried Bousko under her arm. She asked Uncle Siroja again what the "true-hands" were, and disdainfully, although with some compassion, he told us, pointing to the neighboring island across the strait.

"They got stuck on the islands around Hydropark, mostly on Truhaniv. Fuck knows how, maybe they were from the downtown neighborhoods, you know, Obolon or Podil and that, and managed to make it over when the washout happened. So, we call them Truhans, cuz they're from Truhaniv Island. They live like wild animals, God have mercy on them. There's no houses there, nothin'."

"So why don't they move over to Rusanivka?" Zoïa asked.

Uncle Siroja looked at her in surprise.

" . . . Cause we don't let them in."

2

Absurd as it sounds, the bribe we handed was in US dollars we'd hidden at home. Apparently, Uncle Siroja believed that the end of the world was temporary. He was waiting for his happy ending after the fallout. He accompanied us into our flat, tactfully coughed into his fist, turned towards the window and started studying the boulevard below with interest. He stood with his rifle slung on his back while we took the money out of our winter boots. Then, touched by our generosity, Uncle Siroja decided to demonstrate his own.

"I'm in charge at the checkpoint until the morning. Head down and take everything you can from the car. I don't need it."

"We've already taken it."

"Don't be stupid. Take the battery out of the car, it'll be useful. I'm not letting anyone out today, but tomorrow people might dismantle it for spare parts. We've brought in generators; I knew where to find them. But who knows what'll happen in the future? How long this funny business is gonna last? The diesel will run out before then. Oh, and by the way, since you're newbies: We issue everyone energy-saving lightbulbs, you sign for them and we take the old ones. Don't turn on anything else, got it? The wattage in the generators is limited. And another thing you'll need to know. All the young lads take turns heading onto the mainland for gas and diesel runs. When it rains or there's fog, the washout is weaker, seems like."

"Seems like?"

"Well, what're you gonna do: we need to get everything we can from the gas stations we can reach. We might have to last the whole winter. God knows. Anyways, I'll put you down on the list later. Also, what's your job? You know, before the washout."

"Ah . . . I worked for the media," I answered, avoiding giving details.

"Gotcha. So you'll be as much help as milk from a billy goat."

"What about me? I used to work for an NGO living off foreign grant money," Zoïa interjected, trying to be cheeky.

Uncle Siroja once again looked at her like he was astonished she could speak.

"Right. You've been good to me, so I'll be good to you. Go to the bridge, take everything you can. Just at night, right, so you don't piss people off. I won't touch your car, I've got standards. But there'll be different people at the checkpoint first thing in the morning. Roger?"

Uncle Siroja turned to leave. I finally dared to ask:

"You didn't happen to work for some sort of housing authority before this, did you?"

"Kyiv Green, cutting down trees. What, have we met?"

"No, no."

" . . . Ok then. Mr. Media, I'll be expecting you tonight."

He left, his rifle catching on the door jamb on his way out. Bousko clacked his claws over the parquet floor. Then defecated. He took a few steps away, limping heavily on his right leg. Head slumping heavy on his body.

Quiet fell.

"You know something," said Zoïa. "Our landlords disappeared in the weathering so now we have our own flat. In the capital city, no less. Lucky us, I guess?"

3

The night was warm and windless. There were more stars out than ever before, as Kyiv was now dark and the smog had dispersed.

I breathed deeply, quietly moving along the middle of the wide, empty highway on the bridge. I walked along the central passing lane, where before the weathering the *djigit* cowboy drivers loved to crash head-on during another reckless overtake.

Silent emptiness: soft rucksack on my back, soft pad of my footsteps. The wind shrouds me in moisture. A clean moisture, with a clean scent.

Uncle Siroja said that in the first days after *it* happened, they were afraid the island would flood. There was no one to watch over the hydroelectric dam upstream. They avoided the flood. So far. The water retreated one meter, rose two, then fell another half-meter, stabilizing. We got lucky. The water was high but did not reach the road. And the Dnipro also rid itself of the green algae that bloomed with a great stink every summer before the weathering. The Dnipro also got lucky.

Raquel loomed dark in the middle of the bridge. I put my pack down. First, I looked to see what I could get out of the main body. Hm—a road map, can be a token for the memories; Zoïa's cartoon-goose-shaped neck pillow.

I opened the bonnet and started removing the battery. The procedure was reassuringly familiar: alongside her usual ailments, at one point electric shocks would run through the car body, so whenever I parked overnight, I would remove the cable terminal to stop the battery going flat. Otherwise, the car wouldn't start the next morning. Besides that, the battery had been stolen twice last year. Some old crackhead started making a living off stealing batteries. One night he was caught and forced to repent on camera, and a video of it was posted on the Rusanivka community Facebook group. Oh, what am I saying, of course it wasn't forced, we never do such things. The thief was "only" publicly humiliated in front of the camera, "asked" to look into the lens and repent before the crowd. It was like that time at the start of the war when a crowd caught Topaz, the pro-Russian goon, on one of the bridges into Rusanivka and forced him into tearful apologies. Anyway, after a year of thefts, I tended to leave the battery on my balcony at night. During this familiar act of using my phone torch for light and unscrewing the familiar nuts, I started whistling, forgetting for a good minute that this was the last time. Cramming the uncrammable, bulky battery into my rucksack, I felt sorry for dear Raquel, my trusty old mare. She would be gutted here on this bridge. In a fit of inspiration, I let down the handbrake and started wheeling the car across the road lanes, pushing hard and steering her through the open window. When I turned Raquel to face the opposite Right Bank, gravity kicked in and the car rolled down the barely visible slope of the bridge, first at a crawl, then sharply accelerating, at which I panicked and jumped inside the car to keep control of the steering wheel. After this run-up I steered right, rolled down the road to the embankment highway, and when Raquel ran out of momentum, I jumped out and dragged her to the statue dedicated to Kyi, Shchek, Khoryv, and their sister, Lybid. The mythical founders of Kyiv.

I slammed the doors and ran back without locking the car. I

did not know whether the weakness I felt was a symptom of the weathering or a result of the physical exertion. I sat another half an hour on the bridge, by my pack. The weakness had stopped. I looked up at the stars. A total silence; not a sound from the Dnipro below. Below me hung a dense blackness, and in this unilluminated Kyiv, just like in the mountains, I could finally see the Milky Way. And, like in the mountains, I finally had time to raise my eyes to the heavens. With melancholic sarcasm I marked how even the end of the world had its bright side. We did not need to pay rent. No more commuting in stuffy packed minibuses. The hamster wheel of two and a half jobs had stopped spinning. The stars seem to flicker more in the city, from the movement of warm air currents. I sighed and grabbed my rucksack straps. The car battery was heavy.

Mr. Twitch stood at the checkpoint. He asked if I had any cigarettes. I sat down beside him to catch my breath. Opposite, at Hydropark, a dozen fires were lit up along the waterside.

"The Truhanovites are trying to get warm," said Mr. Twitch, jerking his shoulders as if a mosquito was getting at his neck. "Soon they'll be completely feral and then attack us like a zombie horde. Buncha waste-of-space hipsters. . . ."

"You mean hippies?"

"Same shit."

4

This is what we found out over the days to come.

Having a stork as a pet is unreal. Not just because it shits where it pleases, and it is easily pleased. Our unfortunate Bousko also happened to be a principled predator; he would not take canned food in his beak.

"It looks like our baby craves live flesh," said Zoïa.

We had never learned how to catch frogs and worms. We begged fishermen for small fish. They weren't too keen to share much, not even small fry. Only with Zoïa.

There was still food on the island. People like Uncle Siroja, who had appointed themselves as the authorities, stood by the entrances of the island's two supermarkets. They regulated the line, checking bags upon exit. The rule from our deprived, post-Soviet childhood, "Max two items per person," had returned. Rations were handed out by the self-appointed authorities: the people carrying weapons. That was why there were few scuffles. A man holding a rifle stood by every water pump. Those in line stayed quiet.

No conflicts had broken out yet. The group in power tended to agree among themselves. Those who ardently wanted to join were accepted into the lower ranks, such as Mr. Twitch on the checkpoint. Old ladies—the people's opinion-makers, as Zoïa called them—were cherished. Besides, people were too weak for strong conflicts. "Grief takes the form of apathy," wrote Conrad. Nearly everyone had lost relatives without even the chance to say goodbye, Zoïa reminded me in a whisper, as we stood in the line. I thought about my mom. I thought about Zoïa's parents. Unlike Zoïa, I did not really think about others, about everyone around me. Everyone in this line for water or food was going through near enough the same thing. When Zoïa mentioned saying goodbye, it reminded me of the funeral of an old classmate who died in a car crash back in pre-Covid times. We were not even that close; we saw each other only once or twice in the years before his death but I was still paralyzed by the thought of how unexpectedly everything can end, for any person. He was not even behind the wheel, and his friend driving was not speeding or passing when the overtaking driver of a multi-ton hulk of a car, of the mine's-bigger-than-yours sort that my old boss used to drive, ended his dick-measuring contest by colliding into them head-on. Everyone in the big car survived, but not in the other. The relatives stood over the coffin, his mother was keening and wailing over it, something I didn't realize people still did now, not in this century—"Oh my little flower, my sweetheart, my little rabbit, my boy, how did this happen?"—and no one knew what to do, and then the priest arrived, for whom all this was merely his job, and even I, an infidel, could feel how much the padre was needed at this moment, how much people needed this ritual of saying farewell, because it was not for the deceased, but for the living, to somehow stop them from falling apart. Because it was so, so it is and so it will be. Organizing the ceremony, the coffin, the death certificate, the graveyard plot, the calls, the invitations, the wake, the restaurant, the money, again nine days later, then forty. When it first happens the relatives fuss, rush around, calculate the costs involved in order to have less time while the time passes until they can apprehend and accept what has happened. To stop them falling apart. I stood by the coffin and I thought how ideal it would be if the priest avoided cliches like, he is at peace where he is now, or about God taking away too early the ones we love the most or, maybe, since these banalities are necessary after all, that the padre would stop talking about the mysterious ways in which our lives' odds are distributed and in fact how common it is to die of a road traffic incident in Ukraine—more than suicide, even.

I thought too much about all of this. But I was not the only one. Uncle Siroja, while instructing me on the new social rules, said that straight after *it*, a few people upped and left the island, never to return. A rumor spread that *it* was not in the least bit painful, even pleasurable. Everyone, to a greater or lesser degree, had experienced the feeling of the weathering: for some tender, for others sweetly pleasant and sexually titillating, for others still the euphoric desire to just vanish. For some, this desire eclipsed their desire to live. I understood them in part. They had been holding on, like in all past times, for their loved ones. For children especially, or elderly relatives who needed care. Or for partners whom it'd be egotistical to go and dump. Perhaps these checkpoints that spontaneously sprang up on all five bridges into Rusanivka were not so much there because of the Truhans (since they could only enter from one direction), but because of a half-conscious refusal to simply let people out, never to return. Of course, there were also low food supplies. Uncle Siroja was thinking ahead to spring, when, if this did not end, we would have to plant vegetables on the lawns and roadsides and, if we could haul the soil up there, on the roofs. Yes, the fewer people, the easier it would be to survive, but we couldn't just allow people to die. We weren't animals.

"It's time to set Bousko free," said Zoïa. "He won't survive with us. He might have a chance this way."

Behind the children's playground built in the shape of a little boat, there was a round, swampy inlet overgrown with bulrushes, reeds, and waterlilies. It was inhabited with frogs that, at the approach of humans, would slip into the water without raising the smallest splash. There were also shoals of small fry that on sunny days, right under the golden-warm surface of the water, cut around like miniature torpedo jets.

It was there, on the bank of the little inlet, we decided to set Bousko free. Zoïa carried the stork along the boulevard under her arm, and his long, brittle legs hanging below would sway in time to Zoïa's steps. She had made Bousko a better splint for his fracture, tying it with a natural fiber with the hope the moisture would rot it away and, in time, free his leg. When Zoïa carefully lowered the bird on the bank of the round inlet, he hesitated, then, limping on his broken leg, hobbled over to deeper water. Uncle Siroja promised that none of his guys, those older, bearded, big-bellied men who also fostered sentimental feelings about storks, would touch Bousko.

A frog that had been swimming under a large water lily leaf slowly emerged from the water.

5

"Listen, Mr. Media," said Uncle Siroja, as we crossed paths one day. "You used to work for a newspaper, right?"

"No."

"That's what you told me."

"Well, not exactly."

"Either way, I don't need exactly. Stop by an' we'll have a chat. We can't feed people on account of a pretty face, you get me? Everyone has to put in: each according to their ability, as the saying goes."

Indeed, my work before the weathering was kind of linked to the press and mass media, like I said to Uncle Siroja. For instance, there was a period I prepared speeches for the leader of a party in favor of independent Ukrainian governance without influence from our neighbors. I researched facts, put the facts in the required light, formed political positions given to me into coherent texts with theses, and searched for appropriate epithets to express indignation at his opponents' actions. When I later had to promote myself in my CV, I put down "speechwriter." It sounded a bit sexier.

The next day, in the never-fully-built hotel that had been turned into his HQ, Uncle Siroja told me how he wanted to create a newsletter for distribution. For coordination purposes. His words. Agitprop, in someone else's words. My contribution: to unpretentiously and modestly title the newsletter *The Rusanivka Guardian*. We printed it and handed the newsletter out ourselves around the island. We informed people where food and water points were located, what the rations were, where to hand in old light bulbs for LED ones (as mandated). About the mobilization of males for expeditions to the mainland for fuel runs. About electricity reserves and restrictions. And finally, maybe the most important point: instructions on preventing the sewage system from getting clogged up.

Uncle Siroja, an experienced utility worker, was one of few on the island who knew what was where and how it worked. I saw Uncle Siroja transform before my eyes from a typical Soviet janitor (he saw himself as a battalion quartermaster, responsible for the provisions of thousands) into a politician of the "local successful businessman" archetype. Furthermore, alongside household information, in *The Rusanivka Guardian* we always gently yet assertively reminded our readers about the threat from the now-feral Truhans, Truhanovites, Truhanchiks, whatever, of Truhaniv Island. I think that Uncle Siroja genuinely believed in this threat. I think at the same time, somewhere in his subconscious, he understood that an external threat is useful, as a way to flush away negativity, to stop it from flooding us in a quagmire. Again, to prevent our sewage system from getting clogged up.

I was familiar with this from my work for the politician, long before the weathering of humankind. Back then, we weren't the ones who had created the hate either. We subtly utilized and intensified what had arisen before us. It started with hatred for our compatriots from eastern regions, who weren't patriotic enough in our view, and therefore had brought the misfortune of invasion onto themselves. Then the gradient of hysteria fell somewhat, and my boss accepted that it was not *comme il faut* to abhor hundreds of thousands of one's own citizens. Even if they weren't in your voter base. We refocused all our hatred towards the external aggressor. Although later, in the face of a yet more decisive election defeat, we exploded and started hating everyone who was against us. Not through official communications, of course, but through accessible channels where we called our opponents' supporters "useful idiots," "parochial," or even "fifth columnists." Which, as the elections showed, made up the absolute majority. We remained the aggressive minority, to use Zoïa's words. Like Brecht once quipped, the government needed to dismiss the people and elect a new one. We comforted our boss in a similar way: the nation was immature, we said. But whenever I did what my work demanded of me, I felt shame. An insignificant amount, if I'm honest. It was just my job. They actually didn't demand anything from me straight. The whole team understood the brief perfectly without direct instruction and we used our initiative. I then started half-believing those treatises and the messages I was spreading. They were never lies. Just fiction. Not fakes, God forbid. I only gathered the facts and manipulated where the emphasis should lie.

On my first visit to the hotel-cum-HQ, it was clear that Uncle Siroja was a serious survivalist. Boxes and crates were stacked everywhere in the lobbies, rooms, and corridors. Batteries, generators, sacks of soil with the label of the neighboring construction retailer on them. Drinking water in twenty-liter containers. And, of course, sacks of dried buckwheat—a Ukrainian staple. And he had hoarded toilet paper. Tons and tons of toilet paper.

6

"Oh, you've also decided to take part? *Privyet.*"

Speaking to me, in Russian, was my neighbor. He lived on our floor in the flat across the stairwell. We knew he had a five-year-old son with a mental handicap. The two of us, Zoïa and I, didn't know the son's, the neighbor's or the wife's names. Despite for years greeting each other and on occasion exchanging a sentence or two. The exchanges were enough to know that the neighbor was a bit weird: For instance, he took part in orienteering competitions, the ones where you use radios with big antennas. This, in the era of GPS and smartphones. Our neighbor also listened to other countries on long wave radio and tried to start an amateur radio club. This, in the era of 5G. He was a rangy man with a vertical face; all the folds and wrinkles seemed to run from top to bottom. Slightly bulging eyes, always smooth-shaven, always a little sad and lost. Or maybe just away with the fairies. A child in an adult's world. Immediately after the weathering, he went to Uncle Siroja and offered to install a radio transmitter on the hotel roof to let the other islands of civilization know of our existence. He had heard via his long waves that we were not left alone on this earth. *It,* this thing, had bypassed islands of a certain size. Great Britain was weathered off, but in the rest of the British Isles and in Ireland people had survived. At least along the shoreline. The ones who survived, apparently, were those who actively resisted the weathering, who struggled against the euphorically suicidal moods, who got to the water. The smaller the islands, the higher the percentage of people who survived. Our neighbor only knew basic English. He said he also heard Japanese—it sounded staccato, he said, so he might have been right. When back home I told Zoïa about this, we started thinking up who on Earth might have remained. Jamaicans, maybe. Tasmanians. Or closer to home, Sicilians or Corsicans. The Maltese. People on the Greek or Croatian islands. Maybe even closer than that.

"Khortytsia must be one," Zoïa remembered the next day, referring to another, much bigger island many miles downstream of us, where the Cossack fortress and command point once functioned and now remains as an outdoor museum. "Only who'll be left there? The caretakers and the hundreds of people gone camping along the water for their summer holidays?"

Yes, there wouldn't be many people left on Khortytsia. About the same as on Truhaniv and Hydropark. People there by happenstance, or those who managed to cross the bridges in time.

Our neighbor—Kolya was his name—became the electrician in Uncle Siroja's HQ. Kolya was not allowed to build a radio station because, as Uncle Siroja succinctly and pragmatically put it, there was no fucking point. We started seeing Kolya and later his family more often. First at the hotel, then we started going to each others' places. We listened to longwave radio. Only the English language was accessible to us. We could only guess what the rest were. There was not much of this rest, anyway. We managed to tune into a few channels, despite the noise and whistling on the air.

Kolya's wife was called Lyuba, and his ill son was Maksym, but they always called him Maximka. Maximka loved to stand and hold onto his mother's fat leg with both hands while she sat and talked to us, stroking her son's head like a kitten. They were all refugees from the so-called Donetsk People's Republic. Zoïa and I had long suspected this, from their characteristic Donbas Russian accent, especially Lyuba's, and from hidden signs that you couldn't even name if you tried but could detect intuitively. Naturally, back then, in pre-apocalypse times, we didn't ask if they were from there. Those questions don't get asked while passing people on the stairwell. Especially if you were someone who actually supported—or at least did not actively protest—the hate-fest for people like them, aka people "who've only got themselves to blame."

Sometime later that winter, we talked a lot about life before the weathering, especially with Lyuba. She told us that their town was barely touched by the war directly. But they fled after a year of occupation because, as Lyuba said, living there had become unbearable.

I often sat by Kolya in front of the receiver. My English isn't bad, but we just couldn't figure out what had happened to the world. The radio would mention the words "the erosion of humanity," but focused on more current problems. Things were not all bad here on Rusanivka, it seemed. Comparatively. At least there were no killings.

As for explanations about why the erosion of humankind happened, I heard plenty while handing out *The Rusanivka Guardian*:

It was definitely God's punishment for homosexual marriage. The Riders of the Apocalypse were already on their way. Or had galloped past already: brandishing scythes, one holding a pair of scales—the classic.

No, no, it was Matushka Nature throwing off the evil yoke of humanity. If we had only listened to the pagan earthmother Anastasia and read her esoteric doctrine, the world would never have ended. We could have been living in burrows, building kinship homesteads and planting the ringing cedars of Russia. Hang on. The ringing cedars of what now?

Because it was Russia who had apparently tested a new weapon. Over there, that's the direction it exploded, I heard it myself—you remember the wind was blowing south that day? What do you mean, the wind always blows in from the north here? I'm telling you, I remember the exact moment. Well, at least there's one plus-side to the end of the world! The dream of every sane Ukrainian—not those idiots spouting this brother Russia crap or semi-Russian half-wits—has come true. Russia's now one big wasteland.

"Apart from the island of Sakhalin."

"Which is actually Japanese, in case you didn't know!"

No, no, the problem lies with each of us personally. It was Pachamama realigning herself. We should have all practiced veganism, zero waste, and responsible consumption, always Googling brands for ecofriendliness; we should have been buying almond milk cappuccinos in recyclable cups and no lid, using banana-bark stirrers and a paper straw; we should have been avoiding air travel, well, except transcontinental flights, of course, because you know, being a creative you can just take your MacBook with you and travel slowly around Europe, and even if it takes two weeks instead of two hours, what's the problem? Slow travel, slow life. And we should only have been driving electric vehicles and ordering Uber green. If every single person of the one and a half billion people in China, the billion in India and all of Africa did this, then the Earth would not have shaken us humans off the planet. *We are the virus*!

"No, no. They're trying to deceive us. You know well who's gonna profit off the end of the world."

"Who?!"

"Ah, if you don't get it already, then what am I supposed to tell you?"

A plump old man sat on a bench by a block of flats, warming himself in the rays of a still-mild September sun. He wore old plastic slides and shorts. He crossed his stout legs and I saw on his calf a faded, blueish tattoo in the form of an SS sign.

"Ahhh . . . You mean the—Hang on, didn't the Jews also disappear in the weathering?"

"Ha! So who do you think the Truhanovites are, then?"

7

I started having dreams about the Truhanovites. In my dreams they staggered, crawled towards me—disgusting. Truhans, truncated tree stumps, more like rotten hulks than people, swarming towards me. Brown trunks of an unintegrated, powdery mass in which it was hard to distinguish faces or even limbs. Yet there was also something so human in these trunk-like-beings that I couldn't look at them without horror. I turned my face away, squinting my eyes, stepped back, moaning, No . . . no, no . . . But still they crawled forward, I couldn't run away, I shouted, like a spell against this true horror coming towards me: *This isn't a zombie apocalypse! It's a normal one! Just a normal apocalypse!*

I willed upon my consciousness in my sleep. *No, no, stop! We have just been saturated with pop culture*, I told myself. We cannot perceive existence in its raw state, we have lost the ability to perceive reality without pop-culture references. Everything has to look like something else. There are no Truhans. No zombies. Even after the end of the world, we cannot live without having bad guys. We are too used to having enemies. Soon the Truhanovites will be vanquished, vanquished by the sunrise, oh, when will the sun rise? Hang on. The sun applies to vampires, not zombies. What are the Truhanovites then?

The words I heard in English, *erosion of humanity,* started to hiss and moan in the air. It tormented me, not being able to remember where I had heard the phrase. The phrase itself sounded scary in the dream, terrifying, worse than those Truhanovites who had withdrawn under the pressure of consciousness, now instead the zombie hiss, *erooosion of humanity, buzzzz, eroooosion of humaaanity, buzz, buzz . . .* Rhythmically, hoarsely, echoing, with an elastic *buzz* in the word "erosion." Is that them buzzing? The Truhans? They approached, dust falling off their brown, fibrous trunks, and while I was distracted by my search for the remains of my consciousness, a Truhanovite grabbed my shoulder with his branch-cum-arm.

"No!" I pulled away in horror. "This is not a movie!"

I forced myself awake. I was sweating. Zoïa stood above me with wet eyes.

"Bousko's gone."

She had grown to love going for walks before dawn. We both had grown to love walking around the island now that we had the time. Even with the long food lines and the fuel conscription, there was far less work to do. Truly: What are you supposed to do if you don't produce anything? Siroja, to be fair, thought up jobs for people, but they were not obligatory. So people made up jobs for themselves. There was not a single religious establishment on our densely built-up island, constructed by the Soviets in the sixties. This question had been raised many times on Rusanivka community group chats and requests to the local deputy even before the weathering: How can we live without the Church's presence right outside our house? One was only two hundred meters from the island, built illegally in the park. Another one, also illegally built, stood right beyond the footbridge, in another park. A wooden church assembled from pine trunks. *The Rusanivka Guardian* put out a call, and volunteers—strictly volunteers—started crossing the bridge to disassemble this church, drag it over and reassemble it on our side of the bridge. Old people volunteered too, but they were not allowed to cross, that dose of weathering might be too strong for you, grandma, bring the guys some pies instead, you know, as grandmas should be doing. Is this your first time or what?

The two of us, Zoïa and I, went to the pond where Bousko had been living. Then we searched the swamp in the wooded park and the shoreline. There was no body nor live bird.

"Maybe he's flown south?"

"Isn't that a bit early? It's only September."

"So when do they migrate?"

We didn't know. I vaguely remembered they fly away as early as August, comforting Zoïa that his leg must have healed and Bousko had flown off to join his flock. But we didn't know for sure. Questions that only needed two clicks to answer before, now required straining memory and logic, holding arguments and serious discussions that were often inconclusive.

We hoped that no one had eaten Bousko at least. People weren't starving yet. September was warm. Dapples of sun broke through the leaves in the park trees, and when Zoïa and I stepped out onto the furthest little beach, the golden light poured over us.

A young mom and her son were feeding the birds. The two of us stopped. The mother and son blurred into one figure. The woman was petite, she held her son on her hip and with her free hand tossed the bread into the air and gave pieces to the boy. Due to the child's weight the petite woman had to firmly plant her legs wide on the ground and lean over to one side, but this only underlined her diminutiveness and made her more attractive.

"Look how beautiful they both are," I said.

Above the woman and child swirled two separate flocks of birds, never mixing, like water and oil. On the outside, in wider spirals, flew snow-white gulls. On the inside, pigeons anxiously flapped in their own vortex. Beyond the whirlwind of gulls and doves, quite separate and always along a straight line, hurtled gray crows. From time to time one of them would pierce through the bright tornado in an attempt to single out and herd a gull towards the ground, from there forcing him to release his bread which the crow couldn't catch in mid-air.

On the water the mallards waited for their chance. The humble gray females were mixed in among the green-headed males.

The little boy could only throw the bread as far as the ducks or by his feet, where the pigeons, the lumpenproletariat of the bird world, fought for the scraps. The woman threw the bread high into the air.

"Look, each bird has its own strategy," said Zoïa.

Excited by the unexpected bounty, the flocks of doves and gulls tore around in the shape of an upended cone. The gulls descended in a neat corkscrew. The pigeons fell with more of a clatter, then approached on foot. The gulls could settle on the water to compete with the ducks. The gulls were afraid of approaching people, but they were not afraid of water. The pigeons were unable to fly accurately and were afraid of water, but they could sidle right up against people. The woman would periodically sit her weight on one leg and kick out with her free one to scatter the pigeons into the air, since it made her son laugh. The ducks also would dive their heads underwater, wagging their tails, and emerge, surfing back on the wave a second later: first their head settles, gaze set, followed by their bodies. Like Ukrainian folk dancers, ducks can rock like a boat on the water, but the head stays still, stabilized by its neck. One eye is always focused on the food.

The whitish, dove-gray vortex swirled in the cloudless, cool blue September sky. This air funnel narrowed at the bottom, its mouth directed at the petite woman with the little boy in her arms.

"Look how beautiful they are." Zoïa squeezed my hand.

"Let's go home," she whispered.

It took about an hour to circle Rusanivka along the water. Over the many years before the weathering, I only did this once or twice. Now that we had more time, the two of us, Zoïa and

I, would do this circuit twice or three times a day to work up an appetite for each other. It was a guilty pleasure, it being the end of the world and all. Later at home, when I was approaching orgasm, I closed my eyes and above me swirled a whitish, dove-gray funnel of birds, and I soon felt a light, very pleasurable shame. Maybe this was still a side effect of the weathering, like that wild desire in the car on the way back from the mountains. That heightened excitability later expressed itself differently. Hm. What hadn't Zoïa and I tried over the following month or two? Things we could never have imagined before. Or what we knew about purely theoretically before, and that only fifteen seconds after orgasm we were embarrassed to name out loud, despite my saying such to her, without euphemism, only moments earlier. And then we would lie there and pick through the memories of what we had done to each other, with a sensation of sweet shame for feeling so good when everything was so bad. Zoïa called it a *piccolo Decameron* for two, a sexual *quattrocento* in the time of apocalypse.

In mid-autumn Zoïa told me she was pregnant and had been for a while, it seemed.

There were no ultrasounds to establish the exact term. Obviously.

"I thought we couldn't have a baby without help from the doctors," the future father disconcertedly and soullessly reacted to the news.

It was only then that I was overcome with real fear.

Zoïa shrugged.

"Might be we just 'loosened the bag', as they say in the country," she giggled nervously. "Maybe because we saved the stork. A karmic reward."

Aha. I never imagined it to be like this. Not like this at all. Not at all.

First our own flat, and then our long-awaited child. Our dreams were coming true, for fuck's sake.

8

The weathering was weakest before sunrise. In those first days, volunteers would cross over onto the mainland to ransack the nearby supermarkets. There were many teenagers among the volunteers. After their first outing some inevitably gave themselves cringey names, like Stalkers or Nightwalkers. Which not surprisingly I often heard their friends turn into "The Nightwankers." Still, it was kind of cool bringing back a wheelbarrow full of loot at dawn. You felt like a hero. Goodies for everyone—for free! The first people to meet you along with Rusanivka's border guards were those same beatified grannies. Clicking their tongues and calling you things like our boys, our sons.

But every time you went looking for everyone's free goodies, you had to go further and further. When a couple of times some Nightwalkers never returned, the number of volunteers was greatly reduced. That was when the mobilization began.

Kolya and I quickly marched through the darkness and autumn fog. We were all equal, though by then those who were more equal than others had emerged. They did not go out for gas and food. Uncle Siroja valued gas more, as he had a whole hotel filled with buckwheat grain: no one would starve before spring. Kolya and I did not count as more equal, so today was our turn. As we set off for the mainland I was haunted by a memory of taking the cows to pasture with my grandfather in the cool of morning.

"Kolya, is it scary having a child in such difficult times?"

"You think there's a time when it's not scary? It's always scary."

We silently walked several dozen steps ahead. Then Kolya spoke.

"You think I wasn't scared during the war, when me and Lyuba and the baby had to flee from those Russian thugs? And then, when on this side of the front lines some teenage wannabe soldier goes off on me saying I'm a pro-Russian separatist, and you know, I'm too scared to answer and I think, damn, feels like my kid is the one protecting me, not the other way around. And do you think I wasn't scared after that? We spent half a year in an old trailer, which, by the way, was a charitable hand-me-down from Germany, not even from our own government. I'd come back job rejection after job rejection, lie down facing the trailer wall and worry about how I'm gonna provide for Lyuba and Maximka. I could barely force myself to get up in the morning."

"But . . . But what if . . . you know, what if something happens to you? Like today."

"It's just like any other day."

Zoïa took the news that we were expecting extraordinarily calmly. Once more I was in awe of her. I always felt women in general, and Zoïa in particular, were stronger, wiser and somehow nobler than I am. I have been told more than once, usually by women, that I idealize them. Naturally, Freud would declare that this is unconditionally linked with my mother. Jeez, quite the revelation. I was an only child growing up with just my mom and I remember how, before it was just us two, my father, the man, acted and how my mother, the woman, coped. I promised myself that I would grow up and be a different man than my father. But now, as Zoïa cheerfully joked about things, I was panicking. Take today. What if I never came out of this fog? And . . . there was a thought

I did not want to voice, even utter inside my own head: *I no longer had the right to deliberately cross this bridge, never to return.* Not that it would have been very nice of me to do before, but this question of leaving was now no longer egotistical, but superegotistical. And it wasn't like I'd never considered it before the weathering. I thought about it ever since my father left. I still do. But typically, when a real danger appears, like now, like back in the war, when people came to torture you and threatened to shoot you, the idea of voluntary disappearance detaches itself from your mind, and you want to live, no matter what, and you are pumped with new strength. Even during the strongest assaults of the weathering in the mountains and on the road, throughout this tender, light, thoughtless state of joy at dissolution, this feeling of being in a warm bath—a tsunami wave of salvational, sacred anger, rage, and fury would roll in and compel you to struggle against this forced euthanasia, as Zoïa called *it*. It's one thing if I want to go myself, but quite another if someone or something wants me to be gone.

I switched on my flashlight in the darkness. The ray only penetrated a meter or two in the thick fog. Kolya held his rifle at the ready. We walked quickly towards Livoberezhna metro station. As fast as we could.

At the former roundabout intersection, now with zero traffic, a surprise awaited us. A traffic light, flashing yellow in the fog. Nowhere else had lights still shining. Yet here, a traffic light was flashing at us.

My mouth gaped open with delight. I did not see so much as feel the outlines of the streaks of fog. The electric yellow light flashed murkily against the dark-gray backdrop, I almost cried with joy at so much unbelievable beauty.

Stop. This is the weathering talking. Time to move.

Kolya, who had moved ahead as I looked at the flashing traffic light, turned around. A hand signal in the beam of the flashlight: Hurry up.

I stepped off, quickening my steps, and caught up to Kolya. We entered the roundabout where once there were so many traffic jams. To the left of the fog hung a black mass. This was once the Tourist Hotel, which had blackjack and a strip club. Now it was blacker than the night sky.

We crossed the intersection and entered the embrasure between the buildings, a narrow canyon. We dived under the tin canopy. The fog was thinning: We had entered the covered market and moisture could only seep through the sides. The feeling of weathering intensified. Far ahead, the flashlight beam leading from Kolya's hand rested against the wall and created three-dimensional outlines. An iron platform cart, left for us by the previous shift. In order to spend less time away from the island, one group would take out an empty, lightweight cart to start, another would run in after them to finish loading it, and Kolya and I merely had to haul the heavy cart back. Kolya and I would probably have the hardest time physically, but we would spend the least amount of time under the weathering effect. Maybe I was wrong. Maybe we were more equal than others. Because of our proximity to Uncle Siroja.

I walked up to the cart and grabbed the iron bracket shaped like a T. Kolya slung his rifle onto his back and pushed the wagon back. We had to hurry. I could already feel the lightness in my chest and the desire to lie down, relax, and feel intense pleasure. It was probably a nice death if you let off the brakes. I understood those who left and never came back. Only I didn't want that. And not just because of Zoïa.

I immediately started sweating heavily. My jumper was soaked through. We already had to take a break by the entrance to the market.

"What have they thrown in here?"

"Canned food," replied Kolya.

He was pushing from behind, he could see better.

"Another thirty seconds, then let's carry on," I said, wheezing.

In reality, we sat there another full three minutes. We moved on more slowly to save our strength. An uphill climb ahead.

When we came to the roundabout, we saw another group of people in the fog. Noticing us, they froze. We also stopped. Three of them: two women and one man. Or two men and a woman, it wasn't clear. They started staggering over to us, silent.

"Stop!" shouted Kolya, hoarse.

They didn't hear him. Or ignored him. In panic Kolya snatched at the rifle sling and tore it off himself. I probably should have told him not to shoot, but I didn't. A cold river of sweat flowed between my pectorals and down my stomach. The people stopped, soundlessly, in the mist. Then the largest one of them, probably the only man, slowly creeped further. Toward us.

"Pew! Pew!" wheezed Kolya.

He was next to me, I was surprised to see the size of his Adam's apple from the side. Kolya swallowed with strain. I saw the long, vertical cavities along his cheekbones, the vertical creases running from his nose to the corners of his mouth right to his chin. All a sculptor would have to do to mold such a face would be to just run his fingers straight down the clay. Kolya's eyes bulged with fear. His lower jaw muscles clenched beneath his parchment skin.

Kolya raised his weapon.

"Pew! Pew!"

Hm. Not a bad imitation. From afar in the fog, it might seem like he was actually firing.

Or not.

In any case, these three crouched down and backed away on bent knees, quietly dissolving in the mist.

We returned to the cart. Kolya pushed it before I pulled, and the T-shaped iron handle hit me in the backside, right between my glutes and hamstrings. Thrown forward , I almost fell, but put my foot out just in time to right myself and start pulling. We did not even notice the hill that we had to climb before the final slope down toward the bridge, where the cart sped up so much I had to jog to avoid being nearly hamstrung again.

We stopped on the bridge, out of breath. My boxers were wet with sweat, which tickled as it flowed down the inside of my thighs to my knees.

"Kolya . . . We don't have any ammo, do we?"

He was breathing heavily, hands on his knees. The rifle was getting in his way; he pulled it off and chucked it on the asphalt. The rifle gave a dull clatter in the fog.

"I don't even know how to use it," says Kolya.

We laughed from relief.

They were already coming toward us.

The heroic providers were no longer met by grandmothers carrying pastries, but the people with rifles. I called them the guardians of Rusanivka in our *Guardian* newsletter. Sometimes, because of old habits—the defense forces. They signed me and Kolya in, took away the cart and wheeled it themselves along the riverbank toward HQ. It was not for everyone to know how to enter, what was in there, and how much. It was a change from the beginning, when Uncle Siroja half-jokingly assigned people jobs according to the Marxist formula, from each according to their ability. An unofficial hierarchy was instated. Order was ensured by an organized force—people with weapons. Of course, no one had been left to starve as of yet. We weren't beasts.

9

A sleepy Sun shone upon an empty Earth.

It was the time of year when the mornings were pleasantly cool, but the days were still pleasantly warm. Thanks to the nighttime cold, the last of the green algae, which had rebloomed on the Dnipro, was gone. A great tranquillity. Zoïa and I walked along the beach. The water was so clear, the edge between it and the sand was invisible. Looking straight down instead of along the water, you could wet your feet by not seeing the boundary. The sand was now a fine yellow. Like the water of the Dnipro, it constantly changed color, depending on the light and weather.

We trod along step after step. We barely left any footprints behind us. The packed, wet sand sank lightly, crumbling. Right behind Zoïa's feet as she walked, a drier, shinier spot would form for a few seconds. I would catch up and it would have disappeared, once again filling with water. The same thing happened behind me. Like we were never there.

The roads and concrete fields remained, and the animals would still run across these open areas, unsafe and uninteresting to them, until the grass started to grow through the tarmac. Knotgrass was growing through the paving stones. It was good that people had started going out less.

The multistory cliffs remained where, when storms would shatter the windows, the birds could lay their nests. When Zoïa and I were in the Chernobyl Exclusion Zone some years ago, we saw birch trees growing through the shattered windows of the four-story apartment blocks. But what if something like the exclusion zone, left behind without minders, blows up? Have we shown the planet where the safety button is? As long as no nuclear reactor explodes, everything will be well, although not so much for us people anymore. The planet, left to the plants and animals, could become a fantastical landing pad for aliens to hold an expedition. There is only one problem: I am human, not anything else.

From Hydropark, streams of smoke rose. People were burning fires. We could see the navy tarpaulin tents between the bushes. They are there, across the strait, and do not think to hide. I wondered what the Truhanovites thought about us. What names did they call the residents of Rusanivka? Our guardians set up camps with bright national flags right opposite their fires. A power play. The guardians guarded first and foremost the fisherman. From temptation, first and foremost. So that no one fished just for himself, so that no one left without signing out. Fishing had become part of the island's economy. The catch was divided at the discretion of the people with weapons: a portion went to the fishermen, and a portion to the armed men.

In the wooded park we passed two Rusanivka guardians. They sat on tree roots scrubbed clean by the sand carried in by the tide. Each had a rifle on his lap. With no ammo, probably, like Kolya. Only the authorities had loaded weapons. The weapons were likely left over from the war. But no one, now or then, knew how many of them there were. Uncle Siroja also did not know many weapons were left on the other side of the river. If we were rational beings, we would have lived alongside the Truhans. Not on separate islands, but on one common archipelago. They have plenty of boats. We could have sailed between islands, established utopia. We could have caught fish and sunk any weapons that were not fishing rods. We could have sunk them all in the middle of the Dnipro, opposite the Lavra monastery.

The forested islands of the Truhanovites danced with all the shades of the end of October. Some trees had turned yellow, some red, others orange; leaves were falling from some, and on many they were still quite green. The cloudless sky accented this gamut of color with a cold, deep aquamarine that you don't get in summer. The sun added warmth. We squinted and lifted our faces. Zoïa decided to walk a little longer so her back wouldn't hurt later. She had wanted to get pregnant for so long that she had read all the books in advance. Pregnant women often have back trouble. It was best to walk plenty while you still could, apparently.

A familiar couple walked in our direction. Zoïa called them the chilled-out auntie and her chilled-out doggie. A dog and their owner who, as tends to happen, were (or became) alike. Both were cute, a little round, curly-haired and strawberry blonde: Zoïa theorized that the woman deliberately dyed either her own or the dog's hair to look alike. They also acted the same: a phlegmatic focus, each in their own world, unhurried. The lady looked ahead, the dog unaffectedly sniffed at something without diverting off the straight path. If the dog slowed a little, the human turned and waited. I greeted the woman since we saw each other every day. However, she did not recognize us.

"Maybe her facial memory is even worse than yours?" I joked.

"Well," laughed Zoïa, "we aren't exactly as memorable a pair as they are."

I no longer hid it from myself: I really did relish the opportunity to go out and work less thanks to the apocalypse. Apart from the occasional predawn callout to the cow pasture—as I mentally referred to the supermarket trips, reformulating my emotions about it for myself—and apart from bashing out half a page of *The Guardian* every couple of days or so, Uncle Siroja had not invented any other tasks for me.

The volunteers reassembled the Orthodox church that they had disassembled across the river, dragging it log by log over the bridge. The result was a bit crooked, and one of the corners sagged.

"Good for them. Whatever they need to stop them from stirring up any shit," Uncle Siroja good-naturedly commented about the failures of the amateur builders.

At a safe distance from the Orthodox church builders, two Jehovah's Witnesses stationed themselves next to a portable stand. Both wore suits and ties. Handing out somewhat outdated brochures about how the end of the world was nigh. True, the facial expression of one of the Witnesses seemed to say "I told you so." On the cover of *The Watchtower* was a burning city full of skyscrapers that looked suspiciously like New York after the 9/11 attacks. A procession of cheerful people neatly dressed in smart, bright outfits walked out of the city onto green grass. They smiled happily, rejoicing in God's terror. A small girl in a white dress, carried by a carefully shaven man in a beige shirt, pointed out of shot, at the sun. Or at another light source, maybe.

Every morning Zoïa and I would see little groups of people gathering on the riverbank opposite the Lavra Monastery that dominated the skyline on the other side of the Dnipro. The people bowed their heads and made the sign of the cross. Some kneeled, others prostrated themselves, touching their foreheads to the paving stones. There were people younger than Zoïa and me amongst the worshippers. We were surprised to see the chilled-out auntie among them, whom we'd judged a hippie from her appearance. I mean, she was walking around in a hoodie with a big cannabis leaf over the chest. The chilled-out auntie prostrated herself with the same phlegmatic focus she had while walking the dog. The gilded cupolas of the Lavra reflected in the morning sun with a warm pink color. Rose gold.

A little to the side loomed the Ukrainian Motherland Monument. She looked down on us with her cold, iron eyes.

10

A bad scene was stirring on the embankment. People were hanging around the ornamental maples that had just started to redden.

"Let's get out of here."

"Ah, my little misanthrope," laughed Zoïa.

"Incorrect. The term is 'introvert.'"

And we fled the crowd to our glade, to our beachlet.

I didn't want to find out what the crowd was doing. I was feeling good, walking hand in hand with the woman I loved. My head was empty and my legs soft after making love. We had decided that we could start doing it again, if gently and carefully. Zoïa was in her third month, we believed. I carried the food rations now. Zoïa joined the lines, as it was now necessary to come in person in order to receive rations. The lines were getting longer, the people in them more irritable and quarrelling with more energy, having recovered from the first apathetic stage of grief. Uncle Siroja publicly assured them that there was enough food to last a year. From what I had seen in HQ, this was the truth. Maybe. I had just come back from 'seeing to the cows,' as I called it. We had once again brought back a cart full of canned meat, this time from Berezniaky neighborhood. We did not see any Truhanovites.

Uncle Siroja promised to leave me alone for another week. I did not go with Kolya this time, but with Mr. Twitch, who turned out to be my namesake. Kolya had been released from going out to the pasture: he spent his days soldering away in HQ, preparing Siroja's opium for the masses.

The island of the Truhans to the west of us, part of the Hydropark archipelago, once again changed color. The strait now was a vivid navy blue. A light wind raised small waves on the water, seemingly lining up into regular formations like rough diamonds from our shore to the opposite.

The shoreline became more colorful after every night of frost. Many trees held onto their green, but each morning we noticed a new maple that had shaded itself in a hot color, or a new cold-yellow aspen. Or a tall birch that stood out so sharply against the green background that even over a fifty-meter strait, I felt I could pick out every single slender, translucent leaf. The long, winding autumnal shoreline resembled scenery from a Kim Ki-Duk film or something out of a Kawabata novel. A fetish with chinoiserie, Zoïa poked fun at me. *À la coréenne*, I prompted.

We sat on the water-polished tree trunk on the sandy beach. I laid down a thick sweater, folded in two, for Zoïa to sit on. Far in the distance, looking beneath the empty bridge, the strait between Rusanivka and various islands belonging to the Truhans seemed to disappear. If I didn't know better, it looked like I could walk straight there. There would be plenty of space to walk in that light, autumnal forest. Our glade was rather small.

Behind us, a screech.

I ducked from the sharp, high-pitched sound, head tucked down to my shoulders. The two of us, Zoïa and I, turned around. There was a mechanical growl, then a screech and a crack.

"It's a chainsaw."

The sound stopped, but the broken silence was already ringing with shards that scattered like a glass pane smashed by a rock.

Another crash, and a bang, reverberating in our chests.

"Those wankers!" Zoïa ran over.

By the time we arrived, they had already brought down five or six tall and even poplars that grew along the riverbank. They were working with two chainsaws; in a hurry, as though someone might just interrupt them.

Supervising the work were ten or twelve people carrying rifles. The guardians of Rusanivka.

Zoïa almost wept. Anger held her back from tears.

For the first few seconds my ears ached from the noise. Zoïa said something, but I could not hear. I only saw her lips moving. The chainsaw wailed hysterically, its voice lowering to a contralto, then squealing and raising to an ultra-soprano, suddenly cutting off at the last note. A quiet pause, then the crunch and snap of wood. Almost imperceptibly deviating off the vertical, nodding its top to its fellows in farewell, another tall, slender poplar is separated from the others. A subtle swish, and a crash. And a dull thud that reverberates through the soles of our shoes onto the skin of our feet, tickling them.

After the felling, the chainsaws continued to roar as they got down to business. The tree trunks were sawn into half-moons, and then the guardians' haulers, harnessed in tarpaulin straps, dragged these half-moons towards the glass restaurant on the riverfront. The process was led by the largest-looking of these guardians of Rusanivka.

Uncle Siroja appeared. He conferred with this large guardian in raised tones. Then the large man had a go back at him. People stood behind the patchy barrier of armed guardians. Among them we recognized a woman who lived in the same block as us in our building, a small old lady with a yappy Pekingese, Chihuahua, or Pomeranian, I don't see the difference. The witch with the bitch, as Zoïa referred to the duo. The little dog growled at people, even tearing at the other dogs, choking itself in its fury of furies. Its owner had to restrain him, sometimes picking him up off the ground by his chest straps, at which the idiotic dog yipped and tugged at his straps in the air, and from the old witch's general demeanor it was pretty obvious that she and her dog were each as bad as the other ("if not worse," as my mom liked to add). I'd have liked to find out who obeyed whom. She could not, or did not want to, control him. The old lady picked up the dog, and it became an armpit crocodile; when Zoïa and I walked past, he bared his teeth and raised his pig-nosed snout.

"What is all this for?" Zoïa asked the old woman.

The Pomeranian, or whatever he was, barked at her. The pernicious old lady was embarrassed for a second, then launched into an assault.

"Are we supposed to freeze to death, hm? Besides, no one tends to the trees anyway. They could fall on somebody!"

"No one is going to freeze . . ." muttered Zoïa, withdrawing.

We retreated to the sound of the stupid little animal's barking. The witch, as we were both well aware, was part of a group that had been going to Uncle Siroja's HQ, demanding that trees be sawed down for firewood. These people dreaded winter. This woman would drive me nuts every time she received a copy of *The Guardian* from me, always, "How are we going to survive this winter, oh how will we ever survive!"

"Give it here!" shrieked the witch, pouncing on a branch left after the logging. "You old drunk! I'm just a little old woman, give it to me!"

She drove away her competitor with her barking Chihuahua, or Pomeranian, or whatever it was. The beefy Rusanivka guardian leading the logging effort indulgently let people pick up the scraps. The old lady turned to him.

"Young man, could you please help a poor, elderly woman?"

She clamped the armpit croc's jaws shut with her hand, and the dog growled and trembled in its fury of furies. The big gunman called over a smaller guy, who picked up the branch of contention, and the old woman grabbed another one on the way; and then the pair left with two poplar branches that trailed behind them along the ground like long tails.

Zoïa walked home downcast. "It's so unnecessary," she murmured. "Freeze to death? In a brick high-rise? During the nineties chaos years my parents lived in a concrete block and they didn't have heating. Not *at all.* Central Bank went bust, they couldn't get their money, and what turned up later wasn't worth anything. Yes, it was chilly. Sure, it was unpleasant. But it never got below minus thirteen celsius at home, and no one froze to death. These city people are so bloody spoiled! Wait, hang on . . . We're also city people now, I guess."

I wanted to gently remind her that perhaps her parents' flat was warmed up slightly by the walls of their neighbors with central heating, that Rusanivka is more humid, being an island at water level, that it gets bitterly cold here and that it is better to sacrifice poplars than people. Once again Zoïa and I diverged on whom we should feel more compassion for: trees or people. I was speciesist, yes. Even if not to death, freezing is still unpleasant, especially for old people. Even for a mean old witch. But I said nothing, and Zoïa continued to pity the poplars.

"Kyiv Green has taken over the planet! What can you expect from them, when even before the weathering, all their job vacancies were for chainsaw operators!"

Of course, by Kyiv Green, Zoïa meant Uncle Siroja. But Zoïa was wrong, as it happened. Uncle Siroja had not planned to chop down any trees. It was later he pretended as though it happened with his full knowledge.

Besides, the firewood was not hauled over to his hotel-HQ, but stacked up beside the restaurant on the riverfront. This building was separated from the rest and recently had been well guarded by people carrying weapons.

11

Or not. I was wrong. Zoïa did not feel less compassion for people. You could say the opposite: she had a wider circle of empathy. It just included animals and plants as well as humans.

For instance, it was Zoïa, not I, who would help our neighbor Lyuba. That is, Zoïa would ask me to bring them water from the pump. I would also go stand in the ration line with Lyuba and help bring the provisions back. But this was all Zoïa's initiative.

Lyuba's husband Kolya had barely come home for weeks. Uncle Siroja employed him full-time, or mobilized him, I could call it. And Kolya was happy, giggled Lyuba: "See, at least Kolya's nerdiness has finally come in useful! I've bagged a good one, eh? He's kinda weird, not great around the house, a bit maladjusted, but he's a good guy. My little radiohead! Well, you can see that Uncle Siroja's grateful."

A bunch of food supplies, firewood, and even a few jerry cans of gas had appeared on our balcony as well as theirs. Kolya was not greedy. However, this was no reason for Lyuba to refuse her standard ration allowance—her basic income, as Zoïa called it.

Lyuba and I stood in long lines while Zoïa looked after Maximka. He could not be left alone. And I could not be left alone with the child. Even though I was ashamed of my fear, I was always uneasy in the presence of sick people. I couldn't look straight at them because I was scared of staring.

I was thinking about how Lyuba and Kolya managed living with such a difficult son, when Lyuba lightheartedly chuckled in the line, then decided to tell me how Maximka had grown to love Kolya as if he was his own father.

"What do you mean, as if he was his own father? He's not Kolya's?"

"No, of course not. Kolya didn't tell you?"

I was constantly worried and would sometimes panic, obsessively grilling Kolya on what it was like having a child, especially in such difficult times. Kolya spoke honestly about the difficulties of having an ill son, but he never once hinted that the son was not his. I would not have noticed from Kolya's behavior either. Whenever we went for walks Kolya held his, or well, not his, son's hand. One time another, smaller, boy fell over in front of us and started crying. Maximka started laughing, so Kolya crouched down on one knee beside him, hugged him, and gently coaxed him to see the situation in a different way: "Did you see the little boy fall over? He's hurt himself. Do you see him crying? It's not very nice, you see?" And Maximka understood. At least, he stopped laughing. His disfigured face concentrated, and a solemn awareness seemed to form in his small, cloudy eyes, an attempt to fathom, a slow exertion of thought. I felt creeped out then, and out of sympathy I admired Kolya for coping so well with a child like that.

"Me and Kolya have only been together a year," said Lyuba, seeming surprised that I didn't know.

"What about Maximka's dad? Did the weathering disappear him?"

"Is that what you call it?" She threw her head back and laughed so gleefully that people in the line turned to look at her. "Ugh, that scumbag disappeared the moment his sick son was born."

I didn't know what to say. Of course, I could see why Kolya had fallen in love with this Lyuba. If I had ever met someone with pure, sexual charisma, it was her. Despite the fact Lyuba's appearance and behavior were not my type at all, I could almost make out the waves of erotic energy emanating from every movement of her full body, every hand gesture, every word pronounced in her husky voice, every change in intonation as Lyuba giggled, saying that life was actually easier for her and Maximka after the weathering than before they left the Donbas, where she lived in workers' barracks with cracks between the floorboards that let in a draft, where they had to heat the place with raw anthracite, sorting the slag from the coal by hand. In Ukraine, in the twenty-first century.

Lyuba laughed as she compared this past life with her chic, post-apocalyptic one. A kilo of buckwheat every three days, (still) given away for free. Apartment windows without condensation or that let in a draft. Thick brick walls that were (still) warm and dry. And the luxury, once the child had been put to bed, of alone time with her husband in the kitchen. Even if only to drink tea.

Lyuba was semi-literate: one time I saw her write "four thowsund." She had irregular facial features. Coarse manners. Yet, despite all of this, there was something magnetic in her, this inexhaustible energy and *joie de vivre*, both maternal and erotic, and as we talked the men in the line looked at her, and in some way I understood them: in Lyuba, whose name means "love," you could feel an all-encompassing love of being. Her love could encompass the whole planet.

People like Lyuba will restore humankind, said Zoïa.

12

Zoïa was feeling well. It rained that night. The wind blew loudly outside.

We lay under the blanket, cuddling. She laid her head on my shoulder. I stroked her back with the tips of my fingers. An elastic body, elastic skin.

Having dropped off to the sound of rain outside, I dreamed that we were back on the round-topped mountain, in our little hut, and that nothing had happened. It was easier to get confused now that cars no longer ran outside. Then I awoke, and remembered. Zoïa sighed in her sleep and turned her back to me. I lay there a long time, tenderly kissing her between the shoulder blades with the very tips of my lips, so my stubble would not tickle her, and I quietly wept.

In the morning, we saw an ample layer of glossy yellow leaves that had stuck themselves onto the slick black tarmac outside.

"What are they? Maple leaves, or plane? Their leaves all look the same to me . . . Or are they hawthorn?"

"Hawthorn is a bush, you nitwit. Those are sycamores we can see through the window. The ones from the fairytale of the little boy who climbed up a sycamore tree to hide from the snake."

"Speaking of snakes—the mean old witch was complaining

that the tree might fall into her window. I'm worried she might've made it up to turn our tree into firewood."

The militants from our island defense force, the ones who no longer paid much heed to Uncle Siroja, were still felling trees beyond the island's borders for now. After much conflict and negotiations, the guardians of Rusanivka had started taking their chainsaws over the footbridge towards Berezniaky. On the other side of the river, to avoid the effects of the weathering, they quickly chopped down the old willows that hung their switches over the water of the canal. The trees were bright yellow autumn blotches on the muted background of unkempt grass. The tops of the willows blew about in the wind like strands of hair. And now they were being guillotined. One by one, willow by willow. Until on both sides of the canal, toothless gaps of pulled willows yawned.

13

The wind dropped, and overnight the sky's leaden awning dispersed. The sky shone deeply blue between the light, spherical, marshmallow-white clouds that hung over the wet-white fifteen-story building opposite us. Today was a bright autumn day.

Zoïa left the room without her clothes on, and I watched as she moved, taking in every movement. It was already getting chilly, but she loved it when it was chilly. And I loved looking at her naked. Two elongated muscles down both sides of her spine: with every step either the left or the right would tense. The other would relax, as if dissolving in the curve of her lower back, only to protrude once again. It was so beautiful, I observed, to catch the slight jiggle of her thigh in that short moment it tensed to take on her body weight. I wanted to ask her to just walk about, just to follow from behind and observe.

"You are so beautiful," I whispered, when Zoïa returned to the room.

"I already feel my belly rounding," she said. I hadn't noticed yet.

When we went outside, the sycamore leaves on the tarmac turned out to be unexpectedly large up close. Every wet leaf glistened in the slanting sunlight, and every one in its own way. No twin among them, Zoïa and I agreed. The deep-cut contours of each leaf was different. I raised my head. The sycamore reached the fifth or sixth floor. It would be a pity if it were cut down.

We didn't go to the riverfront, but toward the fountains by the canal, which obviously were no longer working. From this side we only had to walk by a few axed willows, instead of passing the whole of the desecrated embankment, where almost no poplars were left. This hurt too much.

Many leaves had fallen. I immersed the soles of my shoes into the largest of the moist piles. They sprang back in a nice way, giving off a pleasant, gentle sound.

Before the footbridge a few old women were trying to sell their old things. *Mink hat, new. Soviet Union* was written on a scrap of cardboard. Coils of wire. Porcelain statuettes of Cossacks in red sharovary trousers and girls in traditional embroidered shirts, hands clasped to their breasts. Bunches of fresh herbs, probably grown on balconies or on the patches of lawn by the apartment blocks.

"Look at this blade," says an uncle of about sixty years old, coaxing people into buying a large knife. "Two handspans. You could stick a boar with that—or a politician!"

He shut up when the paramilitaries in camo appeared. The self-appointed Rusanivka defence force. One time at home, Lyuba confused the correct nomenclature during a conversation, calling them "separatists." Like she used to call the other strange men in camouflage back then, back in the Donbas.

Zoïa laughed: "Careful there, make sure you don't say that outside of this room!"

The Truhanovites were unable to cross the canal from the point opposite this bank, but our defense force still patrolled along it. We walked down to the water's edge. The blue- and yellow-painted cylinders of the former floating fountains still jutted out of the water, but Uncle Siroja had removed the pumps long ago and stashed them away in his headquarters, though he hadn't worked out what to use them for yet.

Every day there were fewer and fewer people outside. We only met one man by the canal. He held a rusty-haired dog in his arms and crooned a song into her drooping ear: "Been waiting for your answer but I've got no hope, a-a-ah, summer is over!"

An aerial battle was being waged above: around the poplars that were still standing, two murders of crows were fighting each other. They chased after each other. Sharply changing their trajectory, flying into the sparse branches, looking for a place to protect themselves, trying to fly up through the boughs towards their enemies; flying off and trying to flee, but seeing there was nowhere to escape. They pecked each other. Feathers went flying. A ruckus of cawing.

And then, from above, sliding down the tall, slick tree trunk, a bloodied body landed at our feet, wings still fluttering. The crow died upon impact. He was dead, tattered, and torn apart.

"Oh God, let's get out of here," groaned Zoïa. "I'm going to be sick."

14

"Where did all the normal people go? Have you seen the chilled-out auntie and her chilled-out doggie recently? Even the old witch stays at home. Doesn't poke her beak out the door."

Not to mention the petite woman and her son we saw feeding the birds. Ordinary people seemed to be hiding away. They stood in the food line and quickly returned home. In contrast, murkier types had crawled out of the woodwork, taken up arms and become the authorities. It was not just Zoïa and I who noticed this. Lyuba, having witnessed this up close before, shrugged. When the old structures are destroyed, new elements seize the occasion. Lyuba put it a little differently: If you stir the cesspool, the shit will rise to the top.

The clouds thickened. The sky showed through only here and there between gray knots of cloud. The two of us, Zoïa and I, walked over the paving stones where the cement had dried in patches. The poplars that had survived the chainsaw ever-so-faintly rustled their dried-up leaves that hadn't yet fallen. The canal water was murky and flat, yet when we walked under the former highway bridge and, instead of the canal, the strait of the Dnipro lay before us, we saw high wave crests breaking on the surface of the water. River water behaves completely differently.

The island opposite us became more beautiful as each day passed. In the cold, in the half-light that condensed darkly either before a sudden downpour or prolonged rainfall, among the contrasting colors, between the yellow and orange bushes, the fires of the Truhanovites kept blazing. Smoke no longer rose from them. Perhaps it was because of the weather. Now we only noticed flickering hot patches. Our militant defenders put a fisherman with a rifle and a blue-and-yellow former Ukrainian flag literally opposite each one of these fires.

Closer to the so-called children's beach, people wearing camo strolled along the water. This was new. And unpleasant.

Something was changing.

The uniform provoked more anxiety in me than the weapons. I don't know whether this is rational or not. The uniform signified an oppression that was organized, thought-out, hierarchical, conscious, and formalized.

"Let's walk back up and go around them," Zoïa said gently, trying to smile.

I don't know how, but Zoïa can often sense what I am feeling, even when we're not touching. She and I climbed up the rusty steps from the water onto the paved embankment. One of the defender-militants sat on the swings in the playground. A boy of around four years of age stood next to him. His son, maybe. Or not. Entranced, the child played with the AK, and the man instructed him on how it worked.

"Oh, that's really fucking cute," Zoïa hissed after we moved away from them.

The clouds grew heavier. They halted right over the island. It felt like the air was dripping with moisture. The sky pressed on us.

Between the layers of the heavy, dark quilt of cloud, an even, rectangular window of clean, dazzling-blue sky opened for a short time. The azure glowed and shone. The two of us, Zoïa and I, were stopped by this beauty. The navy-blue rectangle slowly changed shape, progressively transforming into a trapezoid. Then it closed in. Darkness fell.

We avoided the paramilitaries and went back down to the beachlet. The sand was moist, which made the grains stick together and somehow grow in size. They creaked underfoot. Fallen leaves on the path of the wooded park tensed into a springy, solid layer. Oblong yellowy-green ash leaves, mixed with the significantly larger, brown maple leaves that had begun to rot. We walked down the path along the water, a tunnel between the wet bushes. The water of the strait, invisible to us, slopped quietly beyond the reeds.

Once again, we saw a man in camo between the tree roots. I felt a desire to hide away at home. Like the chilled-out auntie with the chilled-out dog. Like the beautiful lady and her beautiful child. Being outside grew more unpleasant every day. But Zoïa needed it. So her back would not hurt as her stomach swelled.

I remembered the phrase that I had dreamed of in English, "the erosion of humanity" and I suddenly got how the humanity had weathered away from our island, just as humankind had been eroded away from the planet.

That is how I felt. I hoped I was wrong. In a stable society there is at least the illusion of stable rules. But as soon as a crisis erupts, as soon as rules break, you can see clearly how the tacit social contract is reduced to rule by force, even if, as often happens, it is tied to a flirtation with the weak as a visible legitimization of this monopoly on power: so it was with the Varangians who became the Kyiv princes of old in the nine-hundreds, so it was with the gangsters who became philanthropists in the nineteen-nineties, so it is now with our warriors of the post-apocalypse. If you stir the cesspool, the shit will rise to the top.

15

Uncle Siroja tried to contain this influence by adding circuses to his bread.

The island people's republic was still functioning more or less effectively. How, I didn't quite understand. The unfussy food reserves had not run out. There was still running water, which, despite outages, did not disappear completely. Whereas everything that went into the sewer disappeared for good. Electricity, despite restrictions, was available. We did not freeze. True, we had switched to using firewood, and in this Uncle Siroja depended on these new militants (which he did not refer to as guardians), who acted independently. In turn, these new militants depended on Uncle Siroja for food. The rubbish was collected. True, it was just thrown in the Dnipro, downstream. The water washes everythin' away.

One day, which started out fine, Uncle Siroja put on entertainment for the islanders using the able hands of our neighbor Kolya. Having seen the bright morning sky, he sent us on an urgent mission around Rusanivka with flyers printed a few days prior.

Some unexpected problems emerged with these flyers as we prepared them, which made me wonder whether my patriotic politician had lost the elections because of speechwriters like myself.

It would have been better not to scare the people, but gain popularity using simple toilet humor, like our rivals. Lyuba confirmed this opinion. Having seen us struggle with writing leaflets in order to entice people to Uncle Siroja's show, Lyuba snorted: "Just write, 'everyone come and see Uncle Siroja show off HIS . . . ' and leave it at that."

But no, obviously we didn't write that. We were too far removed from the people, Zoïa teased. We rewrote the text again and again. Uncle Siroja remained unsatisfied. Finally, we hashed something out. But the people of Rusanivka didn't exhibit much enthusiasm when we started distributing the flyers and, upon Uncle Siroja's request, thrust them straight into people's hands. The mean old witch asked if buckwheat was going to be handed out that day. The old man with the SS tattoo on his calf, now hidden by his padded trousers that coincidentally people with specific nostalgia for the USSR tend to wear, enquired if we, perchance, were Masons. The Jehovah's Witnesses received the biggest shock when we were the ones to knock on their door, not they on ours. To be fair to them, they still managed to take up half an hour of my time with theological discussion. Until I ran away.

Far fewer people came to the event than Uncle Siroja calculated. True, the witch still turned up and sat in the front row, holding her armpit crocodile and clamping his tiny chops shut with her hand. Empty spaces remained on either side and behind them: it seemed the pair had a reputation.

In the middle of the embankment, with a good (although not Rusanivka's best) view of the Lavra Monastery, there's a wrought-iron gazebo. We gathered the audience here. When Uncle Siroja gave the signal, the mysterious curtains covering the edifices next to the gazebo were removed, and it was revealed that Kolya had managed to assemble large solar batteries. They seemed out of place: despite the fine, sunny morning, Uncle Siroja had been unlucky—towards noon, dark, heavy clouds had gathered, and a breeze had picked up. I convinced myself that the small turnout was due to the weather. It was obvious that it would soon rain. Uncle Siroja started dithering. He called up a priest to speak (a fake one, I knew: He was only a deacon). Wearing a golden epitrachelion, or whatever it was called, the bearded middle-aged man performed several energetic bows in the direction of the Lavra and started some abstract chanting. This seemed to work upon the people. Even the old witch got up from her chair and in response to certain key phrases in the text methodically made the sign of the cross with one hand, having worked out how to keep the dog's snout shut with the other. Unfortunately, this didn't last for long. The religious service turned out to be the briefest part of the program.

The priest pulled out his aspergillum and sprinkled holy water on the solar panels. Then the priest, not Uncle Siroja, who was standing humbly to the side, took off another cover. Here the audience livened up. To the people's surprise was a huge television. And it was on!

The solar cells, I was well aware, performed a purely decorative function: by the water below a TV press van was running on precious gas to power the screen. The satellite antenna was pointed to the sky. What I wasn't aware of was where Uncle Siroja dug all this up from.

It was only then I realized how primitive those long-range radio waves of Kolya's were. After all, satellites weren't gone. People's disappearance from the Earth should not have affected satellite operation in orbit.

Still, even Uncle Siroja did not know what would actually appear on screen when the priest took off the cover. Kolya was still an amateur; he could tune into the only live broadcast he could find.

I looked at the screen. We saw a landscape that clearly had been filmed by a drone. No captions or explanations, no sound even, but I instantly recognized this place and practically clapped my hand to my forehead: When Zoïa and I were wondering about which islands people could have survived on after the weathering, we thought of Tasmania, Sicily, Honshu, Kyushu and Shikoku, Cuba and Jamaica, Taiwan, and even the magical Bali—but we forgot a smaller, yet obvious island, the global stage for most made-up and real apocalypses, at least ever since Hollywood and Fox News have existed. Of course, even after the end of the world, this island must remain the center of the end of the world. Manhattan. Not our residential district of Kyiv, a periphery of the peripheries.

The impostor priest blessed the screen with water carefully, so as not to short-circuit it, and quietly retreated to the background, having fulfilled his function, giving way to the more interesting spectacle. When Kolya turned the speakers on, the dozens of people who had gathered by the gazebo huddled closer, craning their necks towards the screen. They even forgot to keep their distance from the mean old lady. But soon someone moaned, offended: "But they're not speaking our language!"

Uncle Siroja's gaze found me. So I stood to the side and tried to relate to the crowd everything I could understand in broken translation. The shot didn't change (clearly, even New York had technical problems after the end of days), but a continuous news narrative was led against the background of skyscrapers. I don't know whether it was real or fake news, or propaganda. What significance did this have for Rusanivka anyway? I translated news about pogroms in the Irish city of Cork, directed against refugees coming off dinghies from the Isle of Man and Isle of Wight, fleeing the authoritarian regimes set up there (any larger landmasses in the British Isles had completely weathered away, by the looks of it). Meanwhile in Tasmania, announced the invisible newscaster, a treacherous war was being waged against the wealthy and the successful who had found themselves sailing on their honestly acquired yachts at the time of the "erosion of humanity" and were now looking for a place to drop anchor. Tasmania was luring the rich via radio, and when they arrived, they would be given food and water, true, but their yachts would be confiscated for common good, fishing purposes and their well-to-do owners were forced to work just like everyone else! With such anarchy at the fore, our blessed Manhattan preserves law and order, and the small amount of garbage floating around our island will be removed soon, our New National Guard has coped so well with the looters and squatters who wish to settle in empty apartments, that our God-blessed Manhattan, land of the free, home of the brave, is great again . . . Given the circumstances. We are still holding talks with Long Island about their plot allocation for our landfill, but in the meantime, limit your consumption, take your garbage to your neighborhood's designated pier, register your strongest rowers with the National Guard: Gas is scarce, and garbage has to be towed as far as possible downstream. The new governor of Manhattan guarantees that the mistakes of his executed predecessor will not be repeated; we know the direction of the current, and so we can progressively clear our waters of waste, so it can float towards Newfoundland. We also remind you that cases of illegal squatting have once again increased. If you hear any unexplainable noises or notice flashes of light in a previously unoccupied apartment, call your local Neighborhood Watch right away. "We look out for each other!" announced the apocalypse presenter in an optimistic tone.

Drops of rain started to fall. The news went in circles, clearly recorded in advance: once more, the Cork riots, cruelty in Tasmania . . . I prepared myself to translate it more clearly, understanding more the second time. But then, surprisingly timidly, the old witch tugged my sleeve. Looking straight into my eyes, she asked me: "Can you put on "Ukraine's Psychic Challenge"?"

16

The weather improved with the first November cold snaps. The clouds parted, and the mornings nipped the tips of our ears and edges of our nostrils. The sun shone through the surviving alley of poplars by our block, throwing the rhythmic shadows of the tree trunks onto the paving stones.

One clear morning the ghost of Bousko appeared to me and Zoïa by the water. However, the bird that took off noiselessly from the bright autumn bushes was not, as I thought at first, a large, snow white heron, but actually an egret.

In the middle of the canal, gulls bobbed on waves made transparent by sunlight. The small gulls that are actually terns. The water seemed to shine from within. The waves now parted in long, smooth arcs. Every arc passing under the terns would raise the birds up a little, and they would paddle their red feet to restore their balance.

"I was thinking something . . ."

"Hm?"

"That was a really slow eye roll."

"Well, your tone hinted you were about to start broadcasting your profound thoughts again."

"Well . . . not quite. Have you noticed that the water

changes every time we come here? Do you remember the day we got back from the mountains, when these waves were black as anything?"

"Precisely these waves?" Zoïa laughed distractedly.

"It's the same thing with sex," I insisted. "No matter how often we do it, it's different every time."

"Whoa, that was an unexpected turn!"

"If it doth please the lady to laugh, I should be glad."

I walked beside her and thought about how happiness is in the small things. Even now. To be naked together. Or to warm your fingers at home after the freezing cold outside. To look at the sky that also changes every time. To watch the birds. The terns on the water, the sparrows in the bushes. Taste, touch, smell, sound, all these slippery pleasures of the body that one cannot hold onto. When a wave of cool air from the window blows onto the sweaty surface of your body in the summer heat as a bird sings outside, it can ignite an unexpected climax in your brain, call forth a fuzzy and also sharp memory of happiness or the happiness of a memory about a similarly cool wave hitting your body ten years ago, and thus this "changes every time" repeats itself enough to evoke the feeling of familiarity. Maybe it is the transience of these fleeting impressions, which are intangible and uncontainable, that gives them their sharpness and value?

"Maybe," I spoke up. "Maybe one's happiness lies in one's temporality?"

"Haha! What did I say?" giggled Zoïa. "I knew I couldn't get away without any sudden maxims from the depths. How many years have we been together? You see, some things never change."

"No, but seriously . . . Imagine if we never grew old, if we were the same for all eternity. Christian paradise as I imagine it horrifies me. If I went to heaven, I'd hang myself! Tell me, do you think they have cunnilingus up there?"

"How about I phone the Pope and find out?"

"Can you get so hungry up there that when you finally bite into your food, you're moaning with ecstasy? Does it ever happen that you drink too much water, but you manage to make it to the toilet at the last second when you're barely able to hold it? Or are the ecstasies only conceptual? If so, thank you very much. Do you stay the same age forever? Are you ageless? I like getting older and getting old too! I like watching the wrinkles gather around my eyes. Now that I say it, you're getting them too . . . See, soon it'll be clear to everyone that this lady here's all smiles and cackles . . .

"And I like the first gray hairs around my temples. I even like seeing the skin on the back of my hands age. I was humming along to Tom Waits, "the devil knows the Bible like the back of his hand," and I absentmindedly started looking at the back of my hand and realized that, despite the metaphor, I actually didn't know my own hand. Look here: a scar of unknown origin. Then my first liver spot. Two fingers have hair on the back of them, and the other three don't. Here's your proverbial 'knowing the back of your hand.'

"And it's so pleasurable rubbing one hand against the other. Slowly, with focus. Maybe I just suffer from arrested development, but I derive pleasure from the body and from everything the body's associated with."

"You say that now, while nothing hurts yet," she said.

"Maaaybe, but still . . ."

"Ah, there's more?" Zoia laughed

"GET THE FUCK OVER HERE!"

An unpleasant, hoarse voice. Coarse and invasive, like a kick up the backside. Hidden by the flashes of sun shining through the leaves, a man in camouflage stood up from behind the yellow bush.

"Over here, I said!"

Two others were reclining on the ground. Some beer snacks and a half-empty bottle stood on a rug spread between the men in camouflage. Their rifles leaned against nearby tree trunks, butt stocks on the ground, barrels facing the sky.

I felt panic move within me in a meaty knot, like a python.

"Why are you walking round here?" the hoarse man asked.

"Excuse me?"

"Quit playing games. It's not the first time we've seen you here."

One of the other two reclining guardians of Rusanivka, another well-built man, spoke up in an unexpectedly shrill voice:

"Just take them to Mr. Petrovych."

"I repeat," the hoarse one raised his voice. "Why are you walking round here?"

"Gone for a walk?"

"Ha-haaa! Gone for a walk, they say! I see you here every day. Who are you working for?"

"Excuse me?"

"Shut up, your 'excuse me's' are pissing me off. Did the Truhans send you here to sniff about?"

"W-what?"

"Are you dumb? I'm asking you, are you doing reconnaissance for the Truhans?"

"That's mad!" Zoïa exclaimed.

"I'll show you what's mad. Take 'em away!"

"Boys, this is preposterous."

"Don't swear in front of me!"

17

I was afraid they would lead us into the bushes, but no. They led us onto the embankment and then to the chic glass restaurant. Stores of firewood had sprung up next to it, yet wasn't being distributed to the people, in spite of the first cold snaps. Recently Zoïa and I had started avoiding this place, so I was surprised to see that something akin to hard shelter made of breeze blocks and metal had been built up around it. Spikes poked out of the top of the barrier. People in uniforms hung around the place. We were taken inside.

"Mr. Petrovych, we've apprehended two suspicious persons near the checkpoints. They say they were just 'on a walk.'"

The first floor of the restaurant was well heated. The defense forces clearly didn't skimp on firewood for themselves. A blaze roared in the fireplace. A big and muscular man was drinking green tea out of a big teacup. I recognized him. It was the same man who led the poplar felling on the embankment. A clear glass teapot sat in front of him.

"Mr. Petrovych, these two go walking by the river every goddamn day. I bet they know where all our positions are."

"So why have you only detained them now?" Mr. Petrovych calmly asked, raising his eyebrows.

"Well, what do I know? They said they were out walking."

"Oh? What sane people are out walking nowadays?" Petrovych drawled. "Alright, let's find out what's going on. Please, take a seat. Don't be polite."

One of the militants sitting further back stuck his head out.

"Oh, hey, it's you."

It was Mr. Twitch. Petrovych turned to him.

"Do you know him?"

"Yes. He's in one of Uncle Siroja's cadres."

"Aaaah, Uncle Siroja."

"But they arrived here from the Truhans' side. You know, Mr. Petrovych," said Mr. Twitch, twitching his neck, "even back then I thought that was sus. But Uncle Siroja let them in."

"Oh, Uncle Siroja . . . A careless, reckless man," Petrovych smiled so tenderly that it was frightening.

While Mr. Twitch told the story of how Zoïa and I crossed the bridge and then Petrovych interrogated us, I just couldn't pull myself together. He did know that we're the ones who had invented the threat of the Truhanovites, right? Or did he not? Or had we not invented it? I was already doubting myself. Petrovych acted with emphatically good manners. He could sense his power. He sipped his brew while we sat huddled in front of him. He even offered us tea. Petrovych, I think, quickly realized that we had been brought in by mistake. Or did he realize straightaway? He must have known that we were the ones who made up stories about the Truhanovite bogeymen, surely?

Petrovych asked about my relationship with Uncle Siroja. I answered that there was no relationship to speak of, only that I wrote texts for him on a given theme from time to time. Less often of late. One of the paramilitaries referred to Uncle Siroja as "the janitor." Why did I not take a rifle and go on sentry? I was afraid of guns. The militants snorted with disdain at my answer. Our warriors were risking our lives, and you? I went out on the food and fuel runs before we had swept everything up around and it got too risky to go any further. Well yeah, all the guys were doing that, if you're looking for something to brag about. But the Rusanivka defense force is something completely different.

"Mr. Petrovych," snickered one of the gunmen. "Our warriors are stuck here without any women, and look what this chump has got for himself."

He said it as if Zoïa wasn't there. The warriors chuckled. Zoïa flinched, and my heart flew to my throat.

"Seems like he's not interested in taking up arms. It's tits he's interested in." The gunmen started guffawing.

"Stop that now," Petrovych ordered the gunmen.

"We've been married for years," I said.

"What difference does that make?" said a militiaman.

"Stop that, I said," repeated Petrovych. "And what do you want from him?" he continued, turning to the militiaman. "Do you want to force him to carry a rifle? He'd just end up shooting himself the very next day, if he doesn't shoot you first."

"Get him out," agreed the gunman. "And leave us the woman."

"Guys, stop," I gasped. "This is my wife, what are you saying?"

"Yes men, what are you saying?" drawled a phlegmatic Petrovych. "This is a legally married couple. Indeed, they must have a marriage certificate. Is that not correct?"

He winked at me.

"Yes, we do!"

"So go and get it. And the lady can stay with us for now."

"What?"

The gunmen snickered.

"The quicker you bring it, the quicker you can get her back."

"Please."

"We're not going to do anything to your woman."

"Please."

"Enough 'pleases,' it's getting tedious. Who do you take us for? You hear that, boys? He takes us for some sort of rapists! Is that correct?"

"No. No! Let's all go to my place and I can show you the certificate there."

"You don't trust us?"

"I do . . ."

"So kindly stop bartering with us."

"I can't leave her here."

"Listen, you," said Petrovych, revealing his irritation for the first time. "Get the hell out of here. I said that nothing would happen. We're not beasts. Am I right, men?"

18

"Just go."

Zoïa spoke up for the first time in a while. Her voice cracked. I suddenly felt like for the last minute I had also been speaking about her as if she hadn't been there or didn't count.

"See," said Petrovych, sipping his tea.

I almost fell down the stairs as I ran out. I ran, gasping, and hated myself. Especially when I tripped, ran out of breath, and slowed to a walk. I forced myself to break into a run again. I fell on my knee going up the steps into the building and then couldn't aim the key in the lock on my first few goes. The drawer flew out onto the floor when I ripped at it. I took the marriage certificate out of the folder. I ran out without locking the door then turned straight back around to lock it, hating myself, as if those few seconds could change anything. As if the laminated pink piece of paper could magically protect us. I was already back by the statue of Gogol. *Just don't slow down.*

In the restaurant, Zoïa sat opposite Petrovych, silent, arms folded over her chest, as Petrovych slurped his tea and sat turned away from her. Zoïa also had a teacup in front of her, and behind her, behind the glass, the tall poplars swayed in the wind. The defense forces kept their own backyard free of logging.

"Well then, what did I say?" said Petrovych, returning the certificate to me. "And you didn't believe me. You can go. Also, your woman isn't too talkative, is she?"

Zoïa sat there, gray.

"How are you?"

"Fine."

Her voice was also gray.

"Don't go walking up that way anymore," ordered Petrovych, and waved a hand for us to be led out.

Downstairs I took Zoïa's hand, and her palm was lifeless, like a dead fish. I hated myself. I hated them. No matter what they claimed, they had fucked us both. I failed to protect her. And she experienced that. She hates me. From the time I ran out until I returned, seven minutes had passed that changed us forever.

"How are you?"

"I said, I'm fine."

A nauseous feeling. Only I didn't know what I could have done differently. What can an unarmed man do in the face of an armed gang?

Zoïa did not talk about it. We mostly stopped going outside. Nothing had happened, and everything had happened. What had she experienced there? Seven minutes in a room full of men who felt impunity and absolute power. Alone. I watched her face, her movements; I tried to guess her thoughts. I didn't even know if I could hug her anymore. Zoïa started spending most of her time with Lyuba and Maximka. I felt it would have been better to talk it out, shout it out, but Zoïa had turned and stayed gray, colorless and lifeless. Lyuba understood that something bad had happened. She once asked if we had had a fight. If only.

One time Zoïa and I boiled tea on the camping stove and tried to warm up. Slowly, with effort, Zoïa wiped her forehead with her hand, and slowly, as if having trouble sifting through her thoughts, she announced:

"So, I'm your property."

"Zoïa, love."

"No, it's fine. It's saved me. Thus far."

"What did they say to you?"

"Nothing."

"Did you tell him you were pregnant?"

"Really?! It's not his business."

"So, what? They didn't say anything at all?"

"Jeez. What do you want to know? They talked about firewood. Between themselves. The big fella just went on at me about the coming winter."

"And that was it?"

"He was just enjoying the feeling of his power," she slowly pronounced the words. "People like that exist. Didn't you know?"

She was transferring her hatred onto me. We didn't feel like us anymore . . . I don't know. What could I have done differently?

HORDE

1

When Uncle Siroja got blown up in his own headquarters, everyone immediately started saying that it was the Truhanovites who did it. People went to look at the blackened stains around the hotel windows shattered by the blast.

The beginning of winter was upon us. The water had not frozen yet. The black water slowly flowed past the island.

Three days later, Petrovych organized an evening funeral for Uncle Siroja. Ten times as many people came to the funeral than to the Manhattan broadcast a month prior. Petrovych did not go through the hassle of distributing leaflets. His men did not hand out invites, but orders. Zoïa didn't go, staying behind with our neighbors' child. I went to the funeral with Kolya and Lyuba.

The priest was the same one who had blessed the solar panels and TV screen with holy water. The open coffin was placed on three stools inside the wrought-iron gazebo on the embankment. With a view onto the island of the Truhans.

Uncle Siroja's corpse did not look severely disfigured, although his face seemed to have burns on the side furthest from us. His abdomen protruded above the sides of the coffin.

Kolya quietly snivelled next to me.

"As if the weathering . . . wasn't enough . . . We're fighting among ourselves . . ."

He was the only one crying at that funeral. Lyuba had her arm around his waist.

Three paramilitaries in uniform stood on each side of and slightly behind the coffin. Petrovych addressed everyone from the front.

"The enemy has insidiously struck right at our very hearts. He should know—" Petrovych thrust his arm wide and back and pointed behind himself, and it wasn't clear whether the "he" involved was the enemy across the strait or Uncle Siroja in his coffin, "—he should know that retribution is inevitable. As we have all seen, Mister Serhii Apollovych was a soft person. Perhaps too soft. Perhaps this is why he paid the price. But we must be firm. Our warriors will heighten their vigilance, and it is my personal promise to ensure this. You all know who I once was."

A murmur of confusion could be heard from the crowd, at which Petrovych modestly laughed.

"Let's just say, I have experience with these things. But now is not the time for this, my esteemed audience. The departed would not want his death to be in vain. Is that so?"

"Yea, yea!" came the responses, like at a revivalist church service, and Petrovych turned to the body, now no longer speaking, but shouting: "Comrade! I swear before this audience to continue your work! I swear that I shall not allow our Republic of Rusanivka to be overcome by the horde! There, on their island, they sleep and see our warm buildings, see our guardian angels, and in their sleep they dream of swarming onto our peaceful Republic! They will not have that chance! My brother in arms! Your death shall not be in vain! I promise you revenge! I promise you retribution! I promise to punish our enemies! I promise the unbreakable protection of Rusanivka! To you I swear! Rest in peace, brother. Float to that place where warriors rest . . ."

I thought that float was meant in the metaphorical sense. I was mistaken. It turned out to be completely literal. Six defenders in camo lifted the coffin off the stools and, instead of taking it into the forest, where a few deceased people had already been buried, they carried Uncle Siroja's body down the steps and to the strait. When the onlookers approached the edge of the steps, several moored boats that were bobbing on the water came into sight.

The people present at the funeral observed the procedure from behind the embankment rail above. The fake priest, having read the procession rites, did not speak out against the pagan ceremony.

Without closing the coffin, they placed Uncle Siroja on one of the boats. The pallbearers got on the two others, and after a few minutes, this whole catalogue of ships stopped in the middle of the strait between our island and its neighbor. In the wintry, navy twilight we could discern several dozen Truhanovites coming out to look at the ceremony.

The boat carrying Uncle Siroja's body was steered to point in the direction of the current. The oarsman then got onto the neighboring boat.

The wet snow soundlessly dissolved in the cold, black water.

On the shore, the padre performed his arcane rituals with the incense burner, letting off gray smoke. The boats on the strait rowed a little against the current to stay in place. When, after ten minutes, it had grown sufficiently dark, the men lit two dozen pitch torches that stood around the body, fixed in prepared holsters along the boat's sides. The island opposite darkened in the slow fall of winter twilight, and upon this background an orange oval, floating with the current, carved itself into our memory.

If you were unaware that Petrovych was an agent in the security services before the weathering, you would be forgiven for thinking he used to be a film director. He wouldn't have been the only imagined celebrity: the Ukrainian Security Service once had a chief who could have been a Golden Dzyga Award winner. Next to me Kolya, a peaceful and mild person, sniffed and mumbled about revenge. The furrows of his cheeks were wet from tears.

Then the convoy of gunmen in the middle of the strait held their AKs up to the sky and blasted a few automatic bursts into the air. The only thing missing was an invocation to Valhalla.

But there remained the distracting thought about how, post-weathering, Rusanivka now sent its waste floating downriver. Some of this waste got stuck downstream and was covering the surface of the water in great patches, slowly making its way to the Left Bank of the Dnipro, around the bridges, and to the small islands.

2

Zoïa was becoming a little brighter. Her voice regained its intonation, even more sarcastic than before. She and I still had not talked about what did or did not happen but could have happened. Before, we didn't speak because things were good. After *it*, we didn't speak because things were bad. We talked about the superficial. Which was the same as not speaking.

But then Zoïa seemed to thaw like the earth in spring, even though winter had set in outside. She became more tender. She even started joking again. Straight after *it* came the thought: How could we carry on living? It turned out that carrying on living was possible. We tried not to leave the flat except to go to the supermarket or the water pump.

One day she placed my hand on her stomach, and I felt the child move inside.

"Ooooh," Zoïa inhaled. "I wonder what that is. Is that its knee? Or a really bony bottom?"

Something rather firm underneath her skin moved along my palm. I should have felt awe and elation, I knew. Instead I thought, *What world are we bringing you into?* and was afraid. There was a languid joy, but fear dominated. I didn't tell Zoïa this, of course. But she's not an idiot, she could sense it. Some things are hard to talk through out loud.

It became far harder to keep warm. To maintain hygiene, too. As predicted, the sewer system broke down. It was more surprising that it had held up for so long. People went to do their business on the bridge where plastic portable toilets were set up. Some people cautiously started going onto the ice floe by the shore at night. Whatever was closest. No point on the island is located more than two hundred, alright, three hundred meters from the canal. But some inevitably didn't make it. Wherever we walked, we saw the traces of bodily functions. Luckily, the temperature stayed a little below zero for the whole winter.

"Yuck. Reminds me of the saying, 'spring will show us who shat where.' Except this year—literally," said Zoïa, screwing up her nose.

The colder and hungrier people got, the more Rusanivka hated the Truhanovites. At least that was the impression formed from the hour spent standing in the food line. It was the only subject of conversation. They're on the verge, the devils, of crawling out of their savage foxholes and swarming into our warm (well, warmer) apartments. What are the Truhans living on? Where are they getting food from? I tell you, a horde is gonna mass onto Rusanivka. They are just waiting for the ice to get thick enough to hold. It is just as well we have the defense forces, our guardians.

Petrovych's guardians set up watch stations along the shoreline, then sat at them next to small bonfires. Which, thereafter, the majority of the fuel allowance went to.

3

One morning I saw my first Truhanovite up close.

The wind tossed the poplars against the still-dark sky. A storm had passed that night, and its remnants blew over the island. The gray clouds hung about in wet rags. They quickly changed shape as they were being pulled and pulled in one direction. There were many crows flying over. They cawed in the bleak dawn.

I went out early. For the past few weeks, I had had insomnia. Ever since that episode with Zoïa. I fell asleep fast, trying to find oblivion as quickly as possible, but I would wake up in the middle of the night, in the dark, and instead of returning to sleep I started turning over the sticky layers of thoughts in my head. Thoughts about Zoïa, our baby, the future. Zoïa would breathe quietly next to me, and I would turn about in bed under two warm blankets; I sweated but could not uncover myself due to the cold in the bedroom. After an hour or two, understanding that I wouldn't fall back asleep, I got up so I wouldn't disturb Zoïa's sleep. I would go out on walks. Endeavoring to not go where I shouldn't. Yet if nothing else, moving helped me fight the gloom that alternated with periods of dumb fear for our future life.

The strait had thawed again after the relatively warm night. The ice floe here was constantly undermined by the fast current. In the shallows on the Truhanovites' side, the white, snow-covered ice around the reeds and rushes was interspersed with gray melted patches and the blackness of open water. Blackness dominated toward our shores.

It was there I saw the Truhan. On the shore, face in the sand, arms tucked underneath him, lay a wet, dead little boy. He was about three years old. He had black, wet, sparse hair on the nape of his neck. I could see the skin of his scalp.

The water had half-washed the body onto the shore. The boy lay so awkwardly that it was torture to see. It felt like if someone straightened his limbs he would get better. Straighten his spine, lay him on his side, free his mouth and nose from the sand. Slightly bend those too-straight, short legs. Unstick those twisted arms from under his torso. Anything, just so his pose could look even remotely like a position that small children sleep in!

Even the floppy bend in his neck was wrong.

And next to him I saw my second Truhanovite up close. A rangy, unshaven and thin man, who, kneeling there beside the boy, looked like a broken stork. He was also soaked through, with the same short and sparse black hair as the child in the sand. Only the man's hair had already started to dry and stick together, in black icicles.

Two members of the Rusanivka defense forces, rifles slung on their shoulders, stood over the man and held him up by his armpits, but he did not notice them, he looked at the dead little boy and almost without sound, without halt, he wept. He spasmodically sobbed, not tearing his gaze from his child.

The pair with rifles looked at me, then looked away. And the man just cried—the thin man with long limbs, a long neck, thin shoulders under wet fabric, completely concave, kneeling. The figure of a crippled stork, his fine, straight nose, sunken cheeks, sunken temples. He looked a lot like my Kolya.

And a few steps away from him, the chubby little boy with his face in the sand. The father monotonously sobbed, looking at his dead son. One of the paramilitaries, just as monotonously, shamefacedly murmured:

"Did you have to do it? Did you?"

The paramilitaries tried not to look at the child in the sand. The man did not hear what they were saying to him, he did not hear anything anyone could have said to him, he did not see or comprehend that anyone else was there.

4

Zoïa says that I have become more tender. When we made love, I would pull her as close to me as I could. Only now very carefully. How I wanted us not to have this baby.

No, that's not true.

I did not tell Zoïa about what I saw. She didn't need that. I never told her.

We went to Kolya and Lyuba's together, and their sick son drew my gaze. Maximka couldn't tear himself from his mother. While she talked to us, she would stroke his head; he would hug her leg. Zoïa noticed my gazes and interpreted them incorrectly. I felt that I had become an unattainable island for her: She could only spy a small section of my shore from afar, and I couldn't pull her into my interior; she couldn't even swim to me. Like I couldn't swim to her. I also didn't know what she was experiencing in the depths of her own island. When she waited a whole seven minutes for my return, at the mercy of ten strange men. Could I ever not imagine, but know, what she felt? Inside each of us is an unreachable island, each of us may spy only a tiny part of another's coastline. The rest is imagination. Made from stories. That is how it's always been. Yet it has always been, and this is no contradiction, the opposite, only in another sense: No man is an island, entire of itself.

No one is an island, and if a clod of earth be washed away by the sea, the land will be the less. The weathering away of every person is a weathering away inside everyone left behind.

Any man's death diminishes me. The dead three-year old little boy with his face in the sand weathered away a part of my heart. I had incorrectly understood Lyuba's phrase about stirring the cesspool. The shit wasn't isolated to Petrovych and his armed cronies, the shit was in everyone. I had written about the wild Truhanovites. Because Uncle Siroja asked me to. I was just doing my job, correctly performing my assigned tasks. It is also because of me that these islands never tried to unite into a unified archipelago. The dead three-year-old boy from another island washed away a part of my heart, but I cannot convey this fully to others. Even Zoïa. Like how she cannot fully convey what she experienced *that* time, and how she has incorrectly interpreted my tenderness, and how I have incorrectly interpreted the fact that Zoïa has seemed to thaw. There are things that cannot be sent between islands on boats made of words, looks, or touches. But it's much worse when you're too afraid to shout to the next island. Because you are afraid you won't hear a reply. You are afraid that this person won't hear the most important part. Suppose I tried to tell Zoïa about *it*, and she gets distracted, nods, and yawns? Then I would hate her in that moment. Only for a moment, but still. Suppose she begins to tell me about what she experienced *then*, and I ask an inappropriate question that interests me and not her. Then she would hate me in that moment. Only for a moment, but still. And this is us, the closest of people. So how could I know—know not imagine—what that wet, broken man kneeling in the cold sand experienced as he looked at his little son, who has just died and is lying there. The lips in the wet sand. Nose in the cold sand. I repeat, repeat, and repeat it, but I cannot express it, I cannot accept it. And she cannot express her own thing. I do not know and I cannot know Zoïa. She does not know and cannot know me. I believe that she believes that I am tender and melancholic because someone has started inhabiting her stomach. I assume that she assumes. I am afraid. I love and I am afraid. I am afraid to try and swim to the other shore, in case I drown. Every man is an island. No man is an island. Each one of us is an island.

5

"Have you heard the news?" said Lyuba. "The Truhan people have already tried to cross over. The strait between us hasn't even frozen over properly."

For a moment, I hated her. Only for a moment, but still. Lyuba stroked Maximka's head, he was immobilized by bliss, tucked into her side.

Zoïa huffed.

"Are you talking about the man those thugs of ours have held in the water tower?"

"Mhm. They say Mr. Petrovych himself interrogated him. Poor man, I feel for him."

"I can imagine."

"Do you know what name they use over there for us? 'Cuz we're on Rusanivka? *Russkies*. Ugh. Petrovych was livid when he heard it! He says it's the worst possible insult. And it was he who asked. 'I'm just curious,' he said. 'Tell me,' he said. 'Nothing will happen to you if you do,' he said. Of course, 'nothing' happened to the guy after that. Petrovych turned on him, all like, how dare you call us that, I risked my life for you fighting against . . ." Lyuba nodded in Russia's general direction.

"Aha. A Walter Mitty type," Zoïa nodded. "By the way, how do you know all this?"

"Well, Kolya's working there. Kolya love, you didn't tell them?" said Lyuba.

"I just change the lightbulbs," Kolya shrugged "Petrovych says that he'll stop feeding people for nothing. 'If you don't work, you don't eat,' he said. By the way, he mentioned you."

I clenched my teeth so I wouldn't spit with rage. I was more interested in whether he had mentioned the child.

That night an icy rain fell. Blisters of water froze on the pavements and tree branches. Once again, I could not fall asleep. I sat in the kitchen to avoid waking Zoïa. Dressed in a winter coat to avoid burning firewood, or worse, any precious gas. It was thanks to Kolya that, for now, we had enough of both on our balcony. He also made us a little heater and a Primus. Magic hands. A magic person. A person of acquaintances and loyalties. Could I really judge him for what he was doing? Yesterday I asked him, when we were alone—between us two, I said—whether he thought Petrovych could have killed Uncle Siroja (whose death you cried at, I thought, but didn't say out loud). "He could have," answered Kolya, sadly. And now he works for Petrovych and it is he who keeps not only Lyuba and Maximka but me and a pregnant Zoïa with food and fuel. And now Kolya talks about Mr. Petrovych with a distinct respect. Despite this, he called the interrogation of the broken man beyond the pale.

"But it was necessary," Kolya exclaimed that evening, with a shaky and unsure voice. In front of all of us.

"What was necessary?" Zoïa asked, raising her voice. "Beating a confession out of a person who'd just nearly died trying to escape over here, to us? Don't you think that for him, just like it once happened for you two—how did you put it, Lyuba? —life had become unbearable? I don't understand you people. You've lived through the same thing. Put yourselves in his place! Lyuba! At least you!"

Zoïa burst into tears and ran out, back to our flat. I made an apology on her behalf, mumbling something about hormones. Then immediately was ashamed for such an apology.

It seemed that none of them knew about the three-year-old boy. Good. Especially for Zoïa. It was good I didn't say anything. I could tell Kolya, but what would that give him? More blame on his conscience? What was the point?

I sat in the dead of night in the dark kitchen and in a winter coat. The icy rain stopped falling outside. But that was only outside.

6

Early in the morning I left the apartment. Even though I knew it was best not to, I went back to the same place. It was like when you give up smoking and you know it's best not to, but you leave the house and walk to the shop with plenty of time to reconsider, and you still go and buy and smoke the cigarettes anyway.

The river still roared and the nighttime icy rain, while freezing into a blistered crust on the pavements, didn't solidify on the water's surface. Ice was breaking apart ice, paradoxically. The black water, so close to crystallizing, flowed thickly, like liquid glass.

The frozen sand, mixed with the ice from the sky, crunched underfoot.

The isle of the Truhans showed itself through the furious spiderweb of tree branches on the other side of the strait. On our side, the lime trees had been standing blackly naked and wet along the canal for a long while. Only the poplars, though a little rusted, still held firmly onto their frozen leaves.

I found the place where he was buried.

The first time, I placed a square of stones around the site. On the second day, I poked some pegs into the ground. Since then I had gradually been plaiting a living hedge out of willow shoots. Then came ideas of weaving a cover for the grave, at which point I understood I was gradually losing my sanity in tending the grave of a small refugee.

I sighed and raised my gaze, wiping my frozen hands on my trousers. The sun and the glassy water came together in an oily haze. There didn't seem to be any fog, but visibility was so poor that even the closest bridge barely shone through the gray. That day, you could only have guessed that the next bridge, usually visible through the supports of the first one, existed.

I looked over my work. Now nobody would tread on the little body by accident. I knew that I would keep coming and I would keep building on it, reworking, making it more beautiful. Since the weathering, every person in the Rusanivka People's Republic was going mad in their own way. My way was not the worst, I said to myself, and I leaned forward and fixed a twig in the little woven hedge. Now it was more symmetrical.

This beach, where he was washed up, before the weathering used to be informally known as the children's beach.

On my way back, head bowed and warming my frozen fingers in my armpits, I crossed the embankment. I was stopped by Petrovych in person.

"Sir! What, am I supposed to go looking for you myself? Did Kolya not tell you that there's a job for you?"

"He said," I swallowed, "that you had mentioned me."

"Let's go." He nodded in the direction of the restaurant. "We've work for the intelligentsia . . ."

He stepped off, and I did not. Petrovych stopped, turned around and smiled. It was probably meant to represent a tender and indulgent, paternal smile. Intended to cheer you up. Petrovych's eyes were calm. But he had a rifle at his belly, and two beefed-up personal bodyguards standing behind him.

"Oh, don't be a coward! Let's go to HQ and talk. I need soldiers."

"But Stepan Petrovych, what use am I as a soldier?"

"Aha! You're a soldier on the invisible front," Petrovych

quipped, and his ingratiating bodyguards snickered at his joke. "Do you know where I served, back before this nonsense started?"

"Roughly . . ."

"Roughly? I'll tell you smoothly. I was in the K."

"The K?" I asked him stupidly.

"K. See?"

7

It wasn't as bad as expected.

You could say that we were working for good.

You could say that we were helping people.

When the temperature dropped further, Petrovych's people recommenced sawing down trees on a mass scale. Now intense logging took place along both the boulevards that crossed the island, and along its perimeter so that the maximum number of people could hear and see the logging from their windows. And when people came outside, they were distributed firewood "from Mr. Petrovych." Black four-wheel-drive cars were parked nearby, wheeled there by manpower. The cars were loaded up with the same old buckwheat and toilet paper—the two must-have accessories to every end-of-the-world scenario.

People could see out of their windows that handouts were being distributed on the street. So they would come down. A crowd would form. From Mr. Petrovych, we would say again and again as we handed out rations, explaining as we did so that, unfortunately, they wouldn't last long. There were fewer and fewer trees on the island, and buckwheat and paper would soon run out. Not to mention the gas and diesel that provided our electricity. We had to stretch it out until the end of winter. And tighten our belts.

And besides—have you heard the news? The Truhans have been trying to crawl over to our island. Even when the ice is so thin. But winter is still here. We must be strong, we must preserve our unity. And everyone must participate in whatever way they can.

"But how? There will come a point when we will have cut down every tree and burned up all the fuel," said Zoïa when they axed the sycamore under our balcony. "We were doing something similar before the weathering. Cutting down and burning things. But at least back then we created things too, instead of just consuming them."

They were unable to turn me into an effective soldier on their invisible front. I would not spread their rumors while distributing rations. Nonetheless, I was constantly arguing with Zoïa in my head. *Firstly, my dearest Zoïa, they didn't give me much choice. Secondly, I am doing the minimum and show no initiative. I don't even say, "from Mr. Petrovych," when I give out these rations, by the way. Thirdly, at least I am being useful for the people. In the here and now. Moreover, by working for Petrovych—or for the people, and not for Petrovych, one could argue—I am giving food, warmth, and temporary safety from Petrovych's militiamen to us and to our child as well.*

In truth, of course, Zoïa didn't say anything to me. Not even with a look. I was the one who created an external, harsh conscience out of her; I was the one to draw dialogue out of her, to try to convince her, barter with her. I cannot understand how it has happened, but even after radical changes, such as a revolution, war, a pandemic, the end of the world, and a coup, I have continued to do roughly the same work as before.

We, the people working for Mr. Petrovych, sometimes went to people's flats. We brought toilet paper and buckwheat—like lovers bringing chocolates and roses. Not to mention the heavy firewood. The lifts stopped working the day the weathering happened, of course. Today I was met at the door to an eighth-floor flat by an old couple. The old man with thick and pomaded hair, combed back in the fashion of his youth, and the old lady balding, her skull showing through her thinning clumps of hair, which was hard, curled, and dyed the color of plums. She was hunched over and therefore had to turn her head slightly to the side in order to look upwards. The old man had a proud exterior, puffed chest, he stood tall and straight and held himself haughtily. Imposingly. He was one of those people whose beauty merely changes with age, transforming from handsome young men into handsome old men.

The grandpa accepted the rations of food and firewood like they were his own. He calmly showed us where to put them. Two of my paramilitary chaperones even took off their shoes when they came in so as not to dirty the floor, out of respect for the imposing old man before them. First time I saw something like that.

The old lady, however, was appreciative, fussing over us.

"Oh, thank you so much my boys. You feed us, you defend us . . . What would we old people do without you?"

The old man gave her an approving nod. She took a square-bottomed bottle with a glass stopper from the sideboard and poured out a reddish liquid for the defenders.

"Viburnum berry. Homemade, from the before-times."

My helpers shot a questioning glance at me. I shrugged. They joyfully drank it down. And at that moment the old lady seemed to recognize me.

"Oh, my dear boy! You were the one who showed that film. Oh, my dear, could we see it just one more time? Ask Siroja, please!"

My helpers exchanged looks. I had to react.

"Unfortunately, Mr Serhii Apollovych is no longer with us. We were sent by Stepan Petrovych."

"Gah, silly woman," reprimanded the old man. "You went to his funeral. You crossed yourself so much your hand nearly fell off."

"Oh my dear boys! Please forgive an old woman. I don't have my schoolgirl's memory anymore," she said, casually admitting to her faux pas and moving on. "Well, can you ask your Petrovych, our protector, tell him that we old folk are finding it hard without a telly. We don't need anything new, even! We'd be happy with watching recordings of old programs," she said, excitedly taking a step forward. "You know what you should ask him for? That old talk show, 'It Happens To All of Us.' It was such an important program, it raised all sorts of terribly necessary topics . . ."

"Looking at current events, I'd suggest 'Judgment Time,'" said the old man.

"Ah! You and your judges," said the old lady, waving him off. "Don't you listen to him, my dear boys." She turned to the grandfather. "'It Happens to All of Us,' do you remember that program? You used to gasp when you watched it. When that young girl was impregnated by her father? And they did a pregnancy test live on air, because she refused to admit . . ."

We hurriedly said goodbye and left them to enjoy their argument about pre-apocalyptic reality TV.

8

One cold morning in January, Zoïa and I heard the sound of automatic gunfire.

One burst, then the next. Then single shots. Because of the echoing between the high-rise buildings it was hard to determine which side they were coming from. I stopped dead. Again, I was not sleeping. Again I was sitting in the kitchen and waiting for sunrise. It was now too cold to go out. After the pauses summoned by the shots, the crows outside, unsettled, started cawing even more loudly.

A sleepy Zoïa came out to me.

"What was that?"

"I don't know."

"Do you think that's *that*? You know . . . The people from Hydropark?"

"You believe that?"

"No. But what is it?"

"I think if it was *that*, we would have heard more shooting."

We listened. In the breaks between cawing we couldn't hear any more gunshots.

At nine o'clock we stood in the long daily line for food. People were saying that the Truhans had tried it again, that they were freezing, the pests. Far from everyone had heard the gunshots. People asked the gunmen tasked to maintain order. The latter just shrugged.

Having received both our ration allowances, I took Zoïa home, then I dared to leave again, cross the road and go to the iron gazebo where we once buried Uncle Siroja and where there was a good lookout point onto the island opposite.

That January was freezing, but almost without snow. The straits were covered by a now-thick layer of ice. Strips of snow lay only here and there on the ice's surface, and they moved from day to day like sand dunes. The strait was fordable, without a doubt. But there was no sign of movement on the other side. The blue tarpaulin roofs of several of their dugouts could be seen through the trees. How inhospitable it must be there now. It wasn't great for us either and we were inside buildings. I returned home.

"Deer," said Kolya confidently.

"Dear who?"

"The animals."

"Oh. No?"

Our dialogues, held in my Ukrainian and his Russian, often led to confusion.

"Swear to God. They were trotting over the Paton bridge. The Drum told me. He shot them himself—he panicked. You know what he's like. Shat himself, he says."

"The Drum saw them?"

"Well, yeah. And shot them."

"Did he kill them?"

"Missed. Because of the panic."

"The Drum" was actually Mr. Twitch. He now had a new call-sign. He turned out to be a famous drummer, and not a famous speed dealer as I previously assumed. I once asked one of the defense force guys with whom I handed out firewood, paper and buckwheat for details about him, as he knew Mr. Twitch-Drum before the weathering. The man laughed and replied, "No, no drugs. He's just like that."

However, Zoïa and I doubted this excuse that the gunshots were provoked by the "pandemic pause." Why would deer from Pushcha forest or wherever trot through a completely empty city, to then cross a bridge straight into a trap that their instincts would immediately sense? Sure, even if there were deer around, they would be more likely to use the ice to get across. That would be more natural for an animal. Or not.

Kolya then stated that he saw Petrovych roasting something very like a leg of deer in the fireplace at his restaurant. Even though he had said beforehand that Mr. Twitch had not hit the target.

"So what, did you see a leg with hide on it?" asked Zoïa.

"No, but what are they going to do, cook it with the hair on? It had no skin, but there was a hoof. A cloven one!"

"So, you can tell the difference between a venison shank and a pork shank without the skin on it?"

"Its hoof was, you know, cloven!"

"So what do pigs have then?"

"I don't know. I'm a city person," Kolya admitted, backing down. "Why? Do you want me to tell you that they were Truhans?"

"Roasted Truhan leg? Jesus Christ!" Zoïa widened her eyes.

Kolya stopped in shock. He was sometimes as naïve as a child.

"Oh, she's just pulling your leg, my love," purred Lyuba, the peacemaker.

9

Meanwhile, none of the rumors going around the island was confirmed by Petrovych. Either he didn't know himself, or he knew too well and he liked the alarm that had been generated. A week or two later, a powerful explosion went off without warning. In the middle of the day. This time everyone heard it. Moreover, it seemed to go off to the south, near Berezniaky. Then another explosion. From the eastern bank, Tampere bridge. Finally a third, after a pause, on the footbridge towards the Left Bank to the north, where the crooked church had been built.

The noise echoed around the high-rises in such a way that, once again, it was impossible to determine which direction it was coming from. Many people went out into the frosty air, sheltering against the walls, although some stood in the middle of the boulevard that was shorn bald after all the trees were cut down. They stood and looked at the sky. Even Zoïa and I went out onto the balcony. It was only Lyuba and Kolya, as they told us later, who immediately grabbed their child and, without thinking from which direction the blast was coming from, got down on the floor as far as possible from the windows.

"It's a reflex now, you see," said Lyuba.

Petrovych, as it turned out, had blown up three of the five

bridges that joined the island of Rusanivka along its perimeter to the mainland. We, the soldiers of the invisible front, were later forced to say during the buckwheat and toilet paper handouts that the Truhans could have laid siege to us Rusanivkites. The bridges had been blown up for our security.

It was hard to even make up a reason for myself as to why we hadn't touched the two bridges that led west, towards the Truhans' islands. But nobody asked me to explain this.

Besides, the canal and the straits were now firmly covered with thick ice.

I didn't understand the version of the story I was forced to spread as I distributed firewood and rations. Whenever I could, I sabotaged with silence. I pretended to myself that my task was simply to help people. I reminded the people of Rusanivka that the food and fuel were growing more and more scarce and that soon everything would only be on coupons for people who help the Rusanivka Republic. In an indirect way I was reminding them of Mr. Petrovych's mercy, who, for now, was feeding us with that mercy. Hm. No, I didn't say anything like that. Surely not.

But after the bridge explosions our Kolya was crushed, morally.

"So Petrovych had explosives after all . . ."

What is more, he knew how to employ them. In contrast to the fallen janitor king. But that was no proof, of course.

10

Warm, humid winds started blowing at the end of February. Thanks to climate change, spring was coming earlier. People in the lines celebrated. Soon, they said as they queued, the horde would no longer be able to cross the strait. Just a few more weeks, or even days, and we will be safe. Then we'll sow our vegetable plots on the lawns and rooftops, and by next year we'll work out what to do with firewood, we'll invent a "winter vaccine," to use an old turn of phrase. Or, God willing, the weathering will recede. Life will go back to normal. A new normal of course, but nonetheless.

The people in the queues bickered and pushed each other. This was because those who waited their turn left the warehouse almost empty-handed. We were hungry and dirty, we had nearly nothing left at home to warm ourselves, and the cold walls by the radiators bloomed with mildew. Electricity was rationed, switched on according to schedule like in my childhood.

Zoïa and I, Kolya, and Lyuba had firewood and a little food that we, damned collaborators, had stretched and stocked up on back in the days of Uncle Siroja. We were scared to burn wood during the day. Someone would surely turn us in if they noticed smoke coming out of the exit pipe we made leading out of the window. Several times wood had been confiscated off people that way. At night, with my insomnia, I would sit and, to help Zoïa warm up a little, would tend the tin fire burner that Kolya had made us.

Zoïa's belly was now round. We tried not to talk about what would come later. Thankfully, the child was due sometime in May, when the weather would be warmer. We just had to make sure we had food.

11

There was a knock at the door in the middle of the night.

That had never happened before.

I panicked, looking where to hide the wood and wondering who had turned me in.

But by now there was no point in putting out the stove. I kept dead still.

They went away from the door. Went up the stairs, it seemed. A few minutes later they returned and started knocking more insistently. They called my name.

Zoïa sat up in bed, frightened, the blanket up to her neck. I took the largest knife we had from the kitchen.

"You've lost your mind. Put it back," she said.

I carried the knife back and, pretending I was sleepy, unlocked the door. Two men in uniform stood in the stairwell.

"Are you alone?"

"Yes."

They rudely pushed past me. They looked at Zoïa and didn't say anything.

"She's pregnant . . ." I began.

"Get dressed," interrupted the militant.

"Warm clothes and warm shoes," said the other one. "Nothing else."

"What . . ."

"The Truhans."

"What?"

"Just meet us downstairs in five minutes. We don't wanna have to come back up."

They did not come back. My heart thumped in my throat. A good sign that they didn't bother Zoïa. What Truhans? I dressed quickly. Zoïa watched me from the bed.

"I thought it was all an urban legend."

"Me too."

"Be care . . ."

"Yep."

When I came outside, several dozen men had gathered in the yard outside the building. Some of them were middle-aged, others in their teens. The sky had barely started to brighten blue, I could not see clearly, but I recognized a portion of these people. My neighbors. From different sides of our block.

Three or four armed paramilitaries made us form up in the semi-darkness. A few more defenders of Rusanivka quickly checked round the block.

"So where are the Truhans?"

"Have they started an assault?"

"Apparently they're mustering."

"Oh, hey mate, how you doing."

"Hey. Got any cigs?"

" I wish. Where would I get them from?"

"Here's one."

"You little hoarder."

"Can I have one?"

"I dunno . . . I've got to make them last 'til spring."

"You haven't thought of quitting?"

"Says the guy who asked for a cigarette . . ."

"Oh, ha-ha."

"So where are we going?"

More men were coming out of the different blocks, joining our group in the former parking lot. Freezing, we stood like a flock of sheep, shaking from the cold and drowsiness and from fear. Kolya stood next to me. He didn't know anything either. Then they started handing us weapons. Well, weapons of a sort. Kolya had come out with that same rifle with no rounds, a leftover from the times of Uncle Siroja. Later I found out that the rifle was also broken. Not to mention that Kolya still didn't know how to fire a weapon. They foisted a shovel on me, which had "Kyiv Green" painted on the handle. Other people were given similar things: hoes, spades. The defenders had clearly broken the locks and gutted the shed where the utility workers used to keep their tools. Some people ended up with a crowbar—others, a rake. It was a peasants' revolt. Torches and pitchforks.

We had been forming up for more than half an hour; the lethargic March sunrise was drawing out our gray faces in a way that was reminiscent of color settings being changed on an editing app.

"Advance!" ordered one of the men in uniform.

12

We stepped onto Rusanivka's embankment. A crow sat on Gogol's bronze head.

Several other armed shepherds, driven out from the other farmyards like ours, joined us. We descended into the woodline. That night the temperature had fallen below zero again; the brown leaves covered in a puff of hoarfrost had frozen in the sand paths. Kolya moved next to me, head bowed on his long neck.

"Oh dear, I wonder how Lyuba is over there without me . . ." he sighed. "Those pricks woke up Maximka in the middle of the night. He had a full-on tantrum when I left."

Jeez. I knew what he referred to: several times I had been witness to their child who, upon separation from his caregivers, would hit himself over the head with all his might, biting and scratching his parents and howling. It was dreadful. Whenever Lyuba couldn't manage, it was Kolya who could settle Maximka: hugging him, stroking him, clutching him closer, and something in his monotone, flat male voice played peacekeeper for the sick child.

We arrived at the strait. I couldn't see any Truhans. We were formed up into ranks along the riverfront. Three men in camo sent our group to the right.

"Who has a firearm on them?" asked the senior commander.

Several people raised their hands.

"Step out to the front. What about you?"

"Mine doesn't work," said Kolya.

"Come forward anyway, it'll still scare them. Listen up! Before we get to the other side, no one is to fire a single shot. Understood? And when we've crossed over—an immediate strike. Any questions?"

"So what, we're attacking first?"

"*The best form of defense is attack*," he answered, in Russian. "Have you heard that before?"

"Yeah. That's what Bush said about Saddam."

"Ah, you're our smartass are you? Right, I'll send you forward without a weapon."

"I'm not going."

"Ah, you want to sunbathe here on this beach? Enough. We'll follow you from the rear. To clear up the deserters. Any more questions? I want complete silence when we cross. I'll fuck you up myself otherwise."

"But it's spring! The ice is thawing, they can't come here anymore."

"Quiet!"

"Shh, grandpa, don't argue with them. Just walk slowly and don't do anything. Just stay close."

"But . . ."

"Maybe it'll blow over."

"Advance!" the senior in camo gave the command.

I watched various groups to the left and right of us stepping off from the trees and moving along the path of sand. A gray dawn broke. Black silhouettes moved in it. I shivered and turned around. A line of men in camouflage, more evenly spaced than ours, followed up the rear. The faces of those right behind me also looked terrified. I think they also knew nothing about this beforehand, I think they were also forced up in the middle of the night, maybe an hour or two before I was. Everyone kept low and traversed over the beach, woodline, and bushes towards the ice sheet.

I tripped and nearly fell, by reflex jumping over the obstacle and landed both feet in a shallow, square pile of snow.

"Stop looking back here and watch where you're going," barked one of the anti-retreat troops to the rear.

It turned out that I had tripped over the small willow arch that barely protruded from under the snow. I recognized it because I had plaited it myself. I was standing with my full weight on the grave of the three-year-old boy. Flinching, I jumped over the little barrier and carried on, and several other people walked over the grave in my wake.

13

The ice was pockmarked. It had thawed and frozen over again several times this year, and rain had fallen on the ice sheet once or twice in the last few weeks. But the ice held firm, confidently: the cold snaps in January and the beginning of February were solid ones. It would last for another week or two. Still, we scattered and spread out so as not to put too much pressure on a single spot on the surface.

We crossed over quickly, quickly shoving through the reeds frozen in the ice, and huddled on the other side. On the isle of the Truhans.

Everyone stopped dead quiet for a second, and only the scraping of footsteps behind us could be heard. And in front of us, the synthetic tarpaulin roofs of their dugouts shone darkly from within the trees.

"Advance!" roared the commander.

A few shots come from behind. I recoil and hit the ground, get up and, tripping over again, jump out of the way of the shots and start running forward, I hear that same command once again and I run forward, and the people in front run past the dugouts, one after another, and the majority of us don't touch them, although some batter at the walls, bringing down the roofs with crowbars and axes, jump on top and trample them. I run past all this and look back, panting, sweat already filling my eyes after these few miserable seconds, because of the sweat the cold slices at my eyes, I don't see anything, the cold is in my frightened, wet chest under my clothes, the self-defense forces are shooting into the dugout homes. Half of the uniformed defenders of Rusanivka, like us, a herd of rams, run past the sleepy enemy, doing nothing, but some people still fire shots.

Kolya, lost, runs toward me with his toy gun. He was more sunken in his middle than ever, as if a black hole had grown in his chest; stooped over, cheeks hollow and black mouth agape. I catch him by the arm and he recoils; he does not see it is me, and when his eyes at last recognize mine, he groans, repeating the same words several times:

"What are we doing? What are we doing?"

I smell smoke, wet ash, and a sour, unwashed smell. We stand on a doused bonfire, all around are rags, rags hung all over the bushes, and behind us in the bushes opens up an entrance into another foxhole that our guys have not noticed yet, being even deeper and more pitiful than the others, almost nothing really, as tall as my waist and covered with earth; I can see the shiny black polyethylene of garbage bags underground, and from this hole crawls out a dirty, squat woman, Kolya stands with his back to her, looking at what our people were committing from afar; his rifle is slung over his shoulder, I jab the shovel in my hand towards him, the shovel prevents me from pointing at the woman in time, I was still out of breath from my run and even more now from the horror of what was about to happen, as the woman raises a dirty axe over Kolya, strikes him, hitting him between his collarbone and his neck. His thick winter clothing muffles the blow and Kolya soundlessly slumps to his knees, his hollow black mouth and facial expression pronounce the same thing: "What are we doing here?" He slowly folds in half like a penknife and drops to his side, I see his clothes grow black, the stain pouring quickly outwards, the woman does not raise her axe again, she rasps, propping herself up off the ground with her axe and her free arm on her knee: "Bastards . . . beasts."

SPRING

1

Spring in Rusanivka is a blessed time of year. Our island looks like a spinoff of Eden. The cherry trees are the first to blossom, followed by the apricots, apples, and lilac. In a different time, you would never have noticed how many fruit-bearing trees we have. These weren't cut down over the winter—too small, perhaps. Or maybe people decided to think with their heads for once.

And the flowers! In one swoop the lawns explode with the yellow fireworks of dandelions, and then you look around and—poof!—those burning constellations have already disappeared, transformed into fluffy nebulae.

And the birds! A small cloud of sparrows flies around a clumsy patch of doves, lands, hop-hopping and carrying away all the crumbs scattered there by an old lady with a little dog. The pigeons can only swivel their stupid heads and watch, shunting their engorged carcasses after them, unable to catch up. The sparrows are already gone. In the woodline the starlings in a glittering, greenish speck rummage through last year's leaves. Big pink jays quiver and skitter in their eternal panic from branch to branch. Titmice flit about. And the nightingales' evening song! It drowns the wooded peninsula, so much it blocks out all other sound. In the mornings, on and over the water, shriek big seagulls. The terns, the little gull-like birds, nervously scoot around the bigger ones. Mallards with smart green hoods bob like little boats along the shore, while the modest, gray females lead six, seven, eight of this year's ducklings behind them. Gray crows interspersed with black rooks show off their aerial acrobatics in the sky, and their miraculously fine motor skills on the ground. I saw the crows steal the terns' prey right off the surface of the water, gut a sealed packet of sunflower seeds, and then a whole murder of them chased a pine marten, three times the size of a crow, up a tree, and systematically slaughtered it: one crow would peck at it, then when the small carnivore turned to face its attacker, another would go for its back. Die, die, die!

Across the strait, the egrets returned. They would slosh about the reeds and—op!—catch a small frog. And—I had to tell Zoïa!—a pair of storks started laying their nest on the stump of a tree felled for firewood, on the island on the other side of the strait. We no longer cut down trees on our side, but on the neighboring island, shipping the firewood back over the river and removing the threat of cold next winter. There are countless trees on Hydropark island, as well as on the larger Truhaniv island next to it. All ours.

Zoïa and I went to look at the storks' nest. It was safe to go walking now that no one stopped us for questioning. Yes, indeed they were storks. Before, in the pre-apocalyptic times, I had never seen storks further south than the villages of Litky or Demydiv, about twenty or so miles away. Whereas now, nature had healed, and they were flying right into Kyiv. And what is more, one of the pair limped on its right leg. Could it be our boy Bousko? Or maybe our girl Bousko? We never did work out which one in that nest was male, and which was female.

She and I, Zoïa and me, walked hand in hand, quietly smiling.

2

At first it felt like life was no longer possible. No one talked about what happened in the days that followed. It was like an accidental drunken orgy which ended in everyone catching gonorrhea. If I bumped into my neighbors, I gave a curt greeting. Not looking them in the eye.

Kolya was given a Christian burial. He was not sent off in a boat. That didn't befit his rank. Lyuba and Maximka stood in the sand where a small cemetery had grown over the last year. The whole ceremony Maximka gurgled and sometimes laughed at the top of his voice: he was entertained, it seemed, by the priest in his floor-length cassock. The rings of smoke rising from the thurible gave him joy. Lyuba gently stroked Maximka's head and reminded him that he had to be quiet and behave like a good boy. He tried, but his mood was irrepressibly joyful. The return of birdsong, the funny smoke rings, and the old guy in a skirt. All for him. Lyuba quietly cried.

Kolya never made it to the thaw, which came less than a week later. The ice started flowing down the Dnipro. The next week it completely melted. And another week later, people started talking.

Standing in the lines, drinking on benches.

The grass started growing.

Either it was the only thing they talked about or it was the only thing I happened to catch, because it was the only thing I ever heard. I couldn't listen to it.

The warmer it became, the more people came outside, and the more they talked.

So how did it happen? Whenever I eavesdropped on conversations, I heard of people pulling those poor creatures out of their primitive dugouts. They saved as many as they could. They protected themselves from foolish, unintentional attacks, deflecting their shots. It was an accident they tried to prevent. Those who were rescued were taken over to our island, given warmth, food and shelter. Memories altered reality. In our memories we create a reproduction, a mental image. When we talk about these memories, we alter this reproduction, this image. And as we recall this image in a collective, we invent a new memory. Then we change it a little bit again. And again. Next, we become convinced that it was exactly as we remember it.

"By the way, were you also surprised about how few of them there really were?"

"I know! We thought there was a whole horde of them. Poor creatures. They were so filthy—the stink! That was also my first impression, I remember. The stench. That was the worst thing: the smell. When I helped that Truhan limp over the ice, I wanted to stuff something up my nose so I wouldn't vomit. By the way, where've they all gone? You think you could identify them by the smell? I heard they've been housed in the hotel, where that dead janitor kept the bags of buckwheat. They've even been given heaters. We're not beasts. Sure. But there's not much food left in the hotel there, I saw with my own eyes. Petrovych transported it all to the supermarket. Though I heard it's running out. Oh well. They've started sowing Truhaniv island. There's an immense amount of land there, hundreds of acres of it. It'll be enough for our island. Those Truhans have already been sent out digging. So what? If you don't work, you don't eat. Sure, pour me some more. Our people are unused to a bit of hard work. Gone soft from city life."

"Yeah, you're right, our people are lazy. Oh well. If they want to live, they've got to get to it. C'mon, don't let the vodka get warm in your hand. Drink up!"

3

At first the sky filled with smoke. Although the winter had been frigid, it also had been snowless —so in spring, the air and the ground were dry. Everywhere stank of burnt rubbish. The peat bogs around Kyiv were probably smouldering again, like every year. It didn't matter where the fires were: the marshes around Boryspil, Bortnychi or even up north by Chernobyl. There was no one to put them out.

Then a dust storm passed over the island. It blew in one night and stayed hovering above us. From that morning the air around us stood still. If we went out to draw water from the pump or get food from the handout points, we had to tie a shawl over our eyes. It grew hard to breathe. The pallid sun barely showed itself through the reddish-yellow, Martian sky.

Zoïa tried to joke to keep her spirits up.

"What's next? A plague of frogs? An alien invasion? By then we'd be over it."

People talking in the food lines said that the old folk were suffocating. Such-and-such's relative didn't wake up one morning. Such-and-such's neighbor died. And then another person crossed the bridge without planning to return. People disappeared, this time deliberately.

"And we're back to this. Life is becoming unbearable, again," said Lyuba sadly.

Is it karma, or is it character?

Lyuba had come back from the handout point with empty hands. They had stopped handing out food for nothing, they told her. Kolya, who "earned it," was gone.

"We can share while we still can," said Zoïa.

Zoïa looked after Maximka when Lyuba went to the warehouse. Then the two of us, Zoïa and I, went down: I was given rations, Zoïa not.

"We've stopped feeding social parasites, only producers," said one of the men in uniform, rifle slung over his shoulder. "You need to earn your food." He looked at Zoïa's belly. "No worries, lady. Soon you'll be back to duty, and then you can earn your food."

He chuckled and reached to pat Zoïa's stomach. I lunged at him and shoved him back, trying to knock him over, but he was stronger and I was blinded by my fury, so a half second later I was lying supine on the tarmac. The defender motioned to hit me with his rifle butt, but he must have recognized me or something, because he just spat on the tarmac by my cheek and said: "No one's going to touch your pregnant woman anyway, you fuckwit. What do you think we are, beasts?"

"I don't know."

He huffed something as he turned away. He left. I sat up. Zoïa crouched next to me, breathing heavily.

"Don't ever act like that again."

"So how *should* I act then? *How*?!"

How should you act when facing an armed man and still preserve your dignity? And the dignity of others? How? Did I make the right decision back then, when I left her alone with the militiamen? No—I was wrong! But this time I was wrong again! Can an unarmed person ever make the right decision when facing someone who is armed?

It would make sense that once the outside threat no longer existed, we could do without a rifle-touting militia. But no. We took down the checkpoints on the surviving bridges. You could go as you wish. If you wanted to leave the island forever, it was now all too easy. Fewer mouths to feed, as one of the defenders of Rusanivka said. Now the defenders had no one to defend against, they made up other ways to entertain themselves. Since the weathering, the cars had remained where they were parked: some on verges, others on the pavement. Their batteries had been taken out long before, the gas tapped. But then they found some handy types to oil and replace the chassis. They cleared the embankment of the debris left by the winter tree felling and they put on drag races along the embankment. It was about a kilometer, maybe more. Well, by drag race, I mean one would sit behind the wheel and another three or four would push the car from behind. Two or three cars could fit side by side in a row. Whoever got to the end first, won. The defenders agreed that they would only use four-wheel-drives. Lighter rides were not allowed. That would be cheating.

An entire social stratum quickly formed, made up of people who lived off these drag races. Mechanics worked the wheel bearings to perfection. Teams of beefy strongmen were brought together as engines. People called them *sonders.* Now and then I wondered, bitterly, whether I should join the sonders. But I didn't have a chance. I didn't eat enough of my spinach. Shame: the sonders were fed well, the best on the whole island. Not just gruel, but meat too.

"And those people dare tell us about social parasites," Zoïa huffed.

As we returned from the food distribution point, we fell behind the cars, but we overtook the old witch with the bitch. The old lady wiped her furious eyes with her fist and swore. That day she wasn't given any rations. Our warriors were risking their lives, but all she had to do was come back with a stamp of a *trudoden* certifying a day's work: she could be sent with the settler party to the former island of the Truhans, for instance. Tree stumps and bushes needed to be uprooted and space cleared for growing. Old ladies usually love scratching about in the soil. Is that not so?

4

When the rains finally fell after the drought they didn't go for half measures. No. The endless downpour lasted over a week. It would ease a little to draw a breath—then hammer down even more. Going outside became practically impossible. We sat in the dark house, half-starving, and ate the rest of the stores that still remained from Kolya's time working for Uncle Siroja and from when I used to work for Petrovych, who, come to think of it, hadn't shown himself for a long time. He was playing puppet master. Or maybe it wasn't Petrovych leading us any longer. Conspiracy theories started traveling around the neighborhood.

The two of us, Zoïa and I, didn't talk much. We had nothing to talk about. That is, we did, of course, but it was better not to. Then it would start: What world was Zoïa bringing our child into? What would come after? A damp patch was spreading outwards from the corner of the ceiling above the window. The wallpaper had started peeling off and sagging. A colony of black mold was growing under the windowsill. We had battled with it all winter and now had given up the fight. Zoïa called the colony our pet.

The storm drains outside had been long bunged up, obviously, and now an ankle-deep river flowed down both the island's boulevards. It emptied into the canal, flowing over the street's surface.

One positive was that this effluence washed away the "who-shat-where" left over the winter, though the piles were now masked by the fragrance of the flowers. The grass now grew up to our knees. Thick, juicy, dark green and sturdy. The wet but cool tropics. Significantly better than the sandstorm and the peat fires of the previous period.

The slim trees snapped under the rain. The thicker ones hadn't survived the winter.

The deluge gradually subsided, but a monotonous rain still hung around to annoy us for a while. It turned into drizzle. The drizzle would hang in the air, settling onto your clothes.

In the evenings, people started noticing some fires glowing in the belltower of the Lavra Monastery, on the Right Bank of the Dnipro river. The first Zoïa and I heard of this was from the old witch with the bitch. In the end, the old witch turned out to be less of a bitch than we thought. She assured us that the Lord was giving us a sign from the Lavra. We went to have a look.

The sign from God looked a lot like an LED light.

Despite the drizzle, a crowd gathered on the embankment. Our defenders anxiously paced around, hesitating as to whether they should disperse us with their rifles.

Yes, no doubt. On the little platform on top of the Lavra's belltower shined an electric white light. Then it went out. After that it flickered in a natural, orange light. It grew. Like someone was burning a fire there, making it as large as possible so it was easier to spot. When the militants decided to disperse the crowd after all, whoever it was on the Right Bank did something to make sure there were no doubters left. The belltower lit up aflame—and fireworks soared above the Lavra. When the rockets were already halfway on their upward trajectory, the first explosion rang out. Then another, and another. The fireworks flew up and up. Red, green, violet.

"How unlike God to do that," Zoïa said to the witch and the bitch when we walked back home. But then the old lady reminded her: pestilence, strife, the Egyptian darkness, and then the flood. Now the fires have descended upon the earth. What other evidence was needed?

When the sun finally came out a week later, it seemed that every single person who was left on the island came outside. I walked down the embankment, holding Zoïa, round as a planet, by her elbow. She had less than a month left to carry the baby to term, according to our calculations. The embankment was chock-full. Teenagers ollied on skateboards and did tricks on scooters by Gogol. On every bench sat a group drinking vodka and eating snacks of non-perishables. Sweaty, well-fed sonders thrust the four-wheel-drives along the swept thoroughfare. Women, with trashy lip implants that made them look like pterodactyls, had somehow survived the apocalypse and came out of the woodwork. People chatted, laughed, flirted. Mothers pushed prams. Children played in the playground.

"It's like the world never ended," said Zoïa.

I also would have liked to laugh and joke, even if it was forced, sour. But I was drowned by a second wave of the trauma of what we had all done in March when we crossed the strait over the last of the ice. The trauma of something that I knew, when I stopped lying to myself, that I had taken part in. Though I hadn't committed violence, I had instigated it. If not on that day, then beforehand. I wanted to believe that I personally hadn't done anything wrong, although I heard everyone say the same thing. No one was to blame, and yet what happened, happened, and Kolya was dead, as was the little refugee boy, and however many more in their hovels that we now cleared and tilled for spring sowing.

5

One morning I did something of which I am still ashamed and of which I will be ashamed until I die. Before dawn, while Zoïa was asleep, I left. The bridges at this time were empty. The two that had survived. I moved south and then east, not towards the Right Bank, but deep towards the mainland, through Berezniaky and further.

I wanted to weather away. I wanted euthanasia. I walked further and further, waiting for that feeling of pleasurable weakness like you wait for the effect after smoking a joint. The empty houses glowed as gray masses. The grass had grown to waist-height, and the trees that no one had cut down rustled in the wind under the pinkish dawn sun. I walked and I walked, past empty yard after empty yard. Several times I climbed over or walked around tree trunks that had fallen during our rainy season, or around great, storm-severed branches. I came onto Darnytsia Square and decided I needed to get further away from the water. I turned onto Myr Avenue. From there, onto Verkhovna Rada Boulevard. There I found poplars toppled over at their roots, so many they'd formed a blockage in one spot. Without people, nature soon takes back what is its own. I walked on and on. After Lisova metro station, at the end of the line, I came to the empty motorway and stepped off from the city. I had to get away from the river.

Finally reaching Brovary, the next town, I felt a certain weakness, but without the expected joy. I sat on a bench next to a four-story building, in the sun. I shut my eyes.

I wanted a drink. Oh well, it would pass. I just needed to go a little further.

What an asshole I am!

I jumped up and rushed back the way I came, gasping for breath, feeling a knot in my convulsing stomach, I start jogging out of fear, my throat dry, I slowed into a fast walk, ok, better just to walk quickly . . . *Well, aren't you the selfish, pathetic little lowlife, these goddamn tortured intellectuals, honestly . . . No, you can't stop now, you've got to keep going! Wanted to disappear, eh? Keep moving, idiot!*

Near Darynok bazaar, at the edge of Kyiv, a pack of dogs leaped barking onto the road. Pinched, hungry stomachs, and pinched, frightened tails. The dogs started to surround me. I looked around in panic and found a piece of gray concrete block. I raised it over my head and started screaming, voice breaking into a falsetto from the fear.

"Get the fuck away! Get away from me! Off! Get the fuck off!"

The dogs snarled and barked. I once heard, and really hoped it was true, that when dogs bark, they won't bite. I hoped that their respect for humans had not completely died over that winter. These were not the same homeless pups from before that would wag their tails and let you stroke them, although they might remember something like this.

If only I had a stick. A big fat cudgel. Or some metal pipework. I search left, right, but remember—don't show them your back, don't run. Back away and shout. Maybe they still remember what people are. Dogs born this year can't be the head of the pack already. The older ones must remember what humans are. There should be some old poles from the old market stalls of the bazaar. But the dogs had come from there. How many more of them are there? No, there's been so much barking, surely they're all here now. But that's their territory: They could go even more nuts in there. In the narrow lanes.

"Oi! Alpha, Milka, heel! Sorry bro. You got any cigs?"

The dogs obeyed even more quickly than domesticated ones. The little angry bitch never listened to our neighbor the old witch.

Two men with messy, long unwashed hair and overgrown beards were walking over to me from the direction of the bazaar. Carrying the exact metal rods that I'd just been praying for.

"Eh look, he's so clean. You from Rusanivka?"

There was a smell about them. To put it lightly. But it was not the smell that made me gasp. I felt my chin start to wobble. *No, stop, they cannot see. Don't panic, don't run . . . Wait, stop, I already said that about the dogs. And these are people. We can reach an agreement. But I have to speak. But my lips are shaking, they'll notice . . .* In the end they spoke first:

"What's going on in Rusanivka? It's wild out there, right?"

"I . . ."

"Don't shit your pants, bro. We get it. You're not the first and you're not the last. We take everyone in, fuckin' do what you want. We're not like you."

"I was just . . . out for a walk."

The pair with messy hair looked at each other and, like in an old-timey comedy, they took a deep breath, leaned back and, after a pregnant pause, burst out laughing.

6

"They've lived over there ever since. As I understand it, they started traveling deeper into the mainland looking for food, and then ran back towards the water. But no one weathered away. They stopped hurrying. They started staying there for longer and now they say they don't feel anything at all. Some of them have been out there for two weeks without coming back. Far from the water, and they haven't weathered out."

"What were you doing out there?" Zoïa said, finally.

"I . . . I was just going for a walk."

Unlike those two, Zoïa did not burst out laughing. She narrowed her eyes.

"Were you planning to leave me alone?"

"No!"

I avoided her gaze.

"Ah, the tortured artist could no longer stand his cruel fate! Is that how it is? So he left his wife and child. Classic!"

"What are you saying?!" I protested furiously. The closer the accusation is to the truth, the more energetically you have to defend yourself. "I just had to check. You remember the fires on the Lavra?"

"But what if you never came back?" said Zoïa. "And why did you go east, not west to the Lavra?"

She believed me easily because she wanted to believe. We didn't talk about it again. As if it never happened.

But it was Zoïa who came up with our wild plan a few days later.

"You said that Raquel is still on the other bank?"

"Sure, that's where I left her."

At that time the drag races were being held on the Rusanivka embankment, and the mademoiselles with shiny silicon lips walked hand in hand with the militants. While some people starved, others were forced to trade their bodies for food. Some people were beaten with a rifle butt for expressing their rage at this inequality, and still others, according to the rumors, had gone over the bridge—and never returned. Once again, I went over the bridge—and I returned. No one stopped me by the hotel with walls still black and smoky from the explosion. On the entrance into Rusanivka dozed a young paramilitary who I knew back when he was one of Siroja's men, but when I walked in he just raised his head, unbothered, and snorted when he recognized me.

"What, didn't like it out there? Come on, uncle. You might as well have stayed there until you got washed away."

7

"Everything seems fine," I reported back to Captain Zoïa. "I get the impression someone might've slept in the car, but nothing's broken. I threw out the rubbish and left the doors open. To get the smell out."

"How are the wheels?"

"That's what I'm saying, everything looks ok. As far as I can tell. The disc brakes have rusted, but we have this problem every winter. I wheeled the car a few meters, it moves."

"Come on Raquel. Don't let us down, old girl!"

"Zoïa, if anything happens, we'll turn back."

"Oof. I hope not."

Lyuba and Maximka were supposed to go with us. Lyuba didn't hesitate, agreeing without deliberation. We, as in Zoïa and I, had already been sharing our food with her for two weeks, because when Lyuba went to the paramilitaries to argue and remind them the reason why she did not have a husband who could provide for her and the sick child, the militants just repeated, food has to be earned, and gave her an oily smile.

Very early one morning, or rather late at night, I went out ahead to get Raquel ready. The battery sat in my rucksack. Each hand carried a jerry can of gas from Lyuba's balcony. The late Kolya was still looking after us all. I walked through the darkness, worried that they might stop and ask me what I was taking off the island.

No one stopped people leaving, but valuable goods might be confiscated.

Luckily the paramilitary guy on duty was sleeping. I crept past him.

And then, sweating from the weight of my load, I crossed the Paton bridge and arrived at the car.

"Come on Raquel. Don't let us down, old girl."

There was not much gas, and the battery had gone half flat. I was not able to turn the car on myself, I was afraid of running the battery down even more, and I sincerely hoped that Raquel would start if we all gave her a push.

I sat on the curb beside the car and waited.

No, I can't do that. I should go and meet them halfway.

8

The sun came out from between the high-rises. It rose straight over the roadbed, above the Paton Bridge. So beautiful. The sun—large and rosy, shining in my face.

Against this background, the silhouette of a pregnant woman. Very pregnant. In her last weeks. The woman drags a little suitcase on wheels. Zoïa and I once spent a long time choosing it on the internet, one that counted as hand luggage for low-cost airlines. A past life. A past-past life.

Next to her waddles a plump woman with a heavy—this is noticeable even from afar—laundry bag on her shoulder. She leads a boy by the hand, a child with somewhat disfigured proportions and movements—also noticeable from afar. He starts whimpering, and at this Lyuba bends down and picks him up, an additional weight to her load.

And behind them limps an old woman, trying to keep up. She drags a trundle cart with one hand and carries a lapdog in the other, tucked into her armpit. Well, that's a turn of events.

"Quiet, Stepan," said the lady to the dog when it yapped at me.

"Everything go ok?" I asked.

"They took my big suitcase," said Zoïa. "Oh well. If we don't break down on the road, we'll have enough food to last. By the way, let me introduce you to Anna Serhiivna, who's decided to join us. Meet my husband."

"Nice to meet you." For some reason I gave her a genteel bow. Where did that come from? I tried not to look surprised at my own self.

"Better take Lyuba's, hers is heavy," said Zoïa, when I reached for her wheelie suitcase.

"Oh, true. Sorry."

I took Lyuba's heavy sack so that she would only have to carry a heavy child.

"How's our dear Raquel?" asked Zoïa as we moved on from the introduction ceremony.

"Still got some spirit in her. Only the battery's died a bit. We'll have to push her."

"No worries, we'll push," said Zoïa, then whispered: "Help the old lady."

I dropped back and with my free hand I took the cart off the old lady with the dog. Anna Serhiivna looked at me with gratitude and then, clenching shut her dog's mug so it wouldn't interrupt, whispered: "You have a wonderful wife."

"I know," I whispered.

Reaching Raquel, we deposited our bags on the pavement. At first, just the two of us, Lyuba and I, tried to push the car. We were not enough. The old mare snorted and stalled. Someone had to stay behind the wheel to put their foot on the gas at exactly the right moment: I was the only one able to do it.

So then, the car was being pushed by a pregnant woman and an elderly lady. One try, two, three. It still wouldn't start.

"I am not going back!" said Anna Serhiivna stubbornly, rubbing a point on her chest near her heart. "Let's give it another go!"

Maximka was left by the dog, who we tied to a road sign pole. The little dog yapped shrilly, and Maximka gushed forth jarring and, to be honest, unpleasant laughter.

Something deep inside Raquel's bowels groaned every time I turned the key in the ignition and finally, on the fifth or sixth attempt, when the women (mostly the mighty Lyuba) had rolled the car a little, it started. Acting carefully, delicately, like trying to light a fire with your last match, I began to warm up the engine. I was afraid of leaving the wheel for even a moment, so Lyuba carried all our bags and loaded them into the boot.

And off we went.

9

We will drive and take our time. Looking for gas stations and shops along the way. And we will get to the little hut on our round-topped mountain. If we have to, we will get there by foot. We hope that we will not be weathered away. There should be enough food for the five of us. Or the six, if we count the little dog. Or the seven, if we count in advance my and Zoïa's child. If everything goes well, then we'll try to live beneath our domed peak, supporting one another and waiting until the water washes away the last remnants of the weathering. We will prepare as best we can, and then we will drive, or even walk on further. Zoïa doesn't think that things had to happen everywhere the same way as on the island, where the erosion of people's humanity followed the erosion of humankind, with armed parasites in power who refused to take care of those in need. Maybe, Zoïa suggests, the island was too small for our community to remain stable. Or too large. Or something just got messed up along the way, which happens sometimes. Perhaps it was because of past traumas; traumas that we had suffered from before the weathering. Because things can be different. And we will drive on, or even walk, and we will finally find a community at the end of the world where, as Zoïa tells me, we will strive to not destroy the world and ourselves. We shall find a community where there is a place for everyone and where everyone is taken care of. We shall find it.

Or not.